a dandelion by

any other name

a dandelion by any other name

Doreen Davy

MENTOR BOOKS

This Edition first published 2001 by

Mentor Books
43 Furze Road,
Sandyford Industrial Estate,
Dublin 18.
Republic of Ireland

Tel. +353 1 295 2112/3   Fax. +353 1 295 2114
e-mail: admin@mentorbooks.ie
www.mentorbooks.ie

Original Edition
Published by Quoin Press, New Zealand in 1998

ISBN: 1-84210-087-4
A catalogue record for this book is available
from the British Library

Copyright © Doreen Davy 1998

The right of Doreen Davy to be identified as the author of this work has been asserted by her in accordance with the Copyright, Design and Patents Act 1988.

All rights reserved. No part of this publication may be reproduced, stored in a retrieval system, or transmitted in any form or by any means electronic, mechanical, photocopying, recording, or otherwise, without prior written permission of the publisher.

Cover Illustration: Kevin Walsh Design, Ireland
Design and layout by Mentor Books

Printed in Ireland by ColourBooks

CONTENTS

1.	All the Bottoms of the World	7
2.	Berry Street	13
3.	To Be a Catholic	25
4.	A Pair of Lying Bitches	37
5.	To Be a Protestant	49
6.	A Dead Unmoving Thing	63
7.	The Blackman	79
8.	Sex Appeal	91
9.	The Friends	99
10.	A Pervert	117
11.	The Beatles	127
12.	The Snogging Grounds	141
13.	'Men Go Mad for Sex'	153
14.	A Celebration	167
15.	Guys and Jokers	181
16.	Homesickness	193
17.	Kawau	203
18.	The Pack	209
19.	Digestive Tubes	213
20.	Arriving	221

What's in a name? That which we call a rose,
By any other name would smell as sweet.

William Shakespeare
(Romeo and Juliet)

1

All the Bottoms of the World

Many people secretly believe that they alone come from strange families while the majority come from relatively normal families, whatever 'normal' may mean. My personal peculiarity, the thing that set me apart, began early in life. The cause was a three-syllable word that followed me around like a deformed shadow. Rammsbottom! We were the daughters of Mr and Mrs Rammsbottom. Our parents seemed oblivious to the sniggering evoked by that name, but then they seemed oblivious to most things.

There was a Stephen Sidebottom from Merton Road who hanged himself. It was the talk of the neighbourhood for weeks, but it didn't surprise me in the least. What else was he to do? At least girls could hope to get married and change their names, but a man is stuck with it all his life. And if he desires the comforts of marriage, he must inflict the liability onto an innocent wife and children.

In the schoolyard or in the street, there were always cruel, heartless lads. Lads in twos or threes, or gangs of them, throwing snowballs in winter, stones in summer, and verbal abuse all year round. These lads used to call me Deirdre Sheepsarse, and sometimes they'd pull their trousers down and waggle their bare bums at me from across the road, calling 'Shaggyarse!' Girls were slightly more considerate. They preferred to focus on the Christian, name saying, 'Oh dear, dear, dear, Deirdre', shaking their heads from side to side as though I'd caused a mess or something. That wasn't so bad.

Lads were brutal creatures and it seemed unfair that my salvation could only be granted by marrying one of them, to rid myself of the awful family name. 'Sticks and stones may break my bones but names will never hurt me' could only ever have been created by somebody with a normal name, like Smith or Jones or Holmes or Harris. A Rammsbottom could never have managed it.

Janet, my sister, and I were happy in our pre-school ignorance. We played together all day in the front parlour making up words to form a language that belonged only to us. The word 'yar' meant let's begin our game, 'ick' meant something was not allowed. There was almost a Germanic sound to our made-up words, although the meanings were different. We had obviously heard the word Rammsbottom mentioned, but not quite realised it was our own unique label, an identity badge we would have to wear to enter the outside world.

Later on, when the awful realisation had taken place, my dad consoled us with the fact that about two hundred years ago there had been a Lord Rammsbottom of Derby, or some such place, and we should be proud to have good blood in our veins. But it didn't impress us in the least. We just felt sorry for Lady Rammsbottom and all her wretched offspring.

He often emphasised the fact that our name had two Ms in the 'Ramms' which made it unique, as though the extra M made a difference. Made it something to be proud of. But it was the 'bottom' that grabbed people's attention. Nobody gave a toss

A Dandelion By Any Other Name

about the extra M.

My dad really was proud of his name. With us being the only Rammsbottoms left in England, and probably the world, my dad had hoped for a son to carry on the family name. My mum told us of his disappointment at each of our births. He even had the name Stanley picked out ready for the long-hoped-for son. Luckily for us he only managed to produce three daughters. Daughters who would one day grab at anybody or anything to change their names.

At school there was an old, crotchety teacher called Miss Higginbottom. She took physical education and I thought I might become her class favourite because of us having something in common – her being a fellow Bottom. But she was just as bad-tempered with me as she was with everybody else. A few of the kids used to scoff at her name too, and asked if we were related. I said we were. All the Bottoms of the world are related through shame.

Around the time I was nine years old I became acutely aware of feeling deprived. The source of my deprivation was simply in being different; I was outside the comforts of the fold. Not only did I inherit such a surname, but my Christian name was also an abomination. In a classroom full of Lindas, Jackies, Susans and Christines, 'Deirdre Rammsbottom' was a double handicap.

'You're too sensitive,' my Aunty Ella would say when I declared my hatred of the family name. My dad's other sister, Irene, said that to have such a name was character building, as though it were some sort of consolation prize. But what nine-year-old girl ever wanted character? To be one of the herd was all I craved.

In my class at school there were the regular outcasts. Fat Pauline; a tall gangly lad called Ian, who had a turn in one eye and whose mother dressed him in tight shorts; a scruffy girl called

Christine Hardman, who often had a candle of snot descending from one of her nostrils, which she promptly sniffed back up if it was mentioned; some lad called Stuart, who stuttered (all the kids called him St-st-st-st st-st-Stuart); and then me with my ridiculous name.

Undercurrents of peer tension came and went, positions of popularity waxed and waned, but the regular outcasts remained much the same. You could tell who the outcasts were when it was time for people to choose teams. Having a Rammsbottom, a stutterer or a Fat Pauline in your team was to jinx it. We were often left like a bundle of unwanted rags in the corner.

Sometimes I reluctantly sat with Pauline for the breaktimes. She was an only child and, like me, she felt lonely at school. She invited me back to her house for jelly and ice-cream, but I refused, not wanting to run the risk of being seen with her after school. I was a reluctant member of the outcast team. It was as though Pauline's fatness might be contagious and I had enough to worry about with my own liability.

Also in our class was a girl who was the embodiment of good fortune. Her name was Lynnette Holmes. She was pretty with blond curls. Sometimes she wore her hair in plaits tied by little tartan ribbons, or she tied it up in a pony-tail forming one ringlet. She had a way of turning her head sharply so that the ringlet bobbed about vivaciously. I watched her and the animated ringlet with intense interest. She wore a pink angora cardigan (mother's hand-knitting of course). 'A nice girl,' I heard one of the teachers saying to another in the school yard as they observed Lynnette, the girl who had it all: nice name, nice cardigan, nice hair.

'Nice' was not an adjective ever used on me. I was tall and thin. My crowning glory was short, straight and mouse-brown with an indomitable cowlick at the front. Janet looked much the same.

A Dandelion By Any Other Name

My mum would implant a clip on either side of our uneven part to hold the thick, straight horsehair back from our eyes; it was the hairstyle of the retarded.

With just eleven months between us, Janet and I looked very much like twins. There was a big mirror over the Welsh dresser in the living room and I spent hours in front of it pretending to be Lynnette Holmes. With pyjama pants on my head, each end tied with ribbons, I would smile and simper at the mirror while flicking the 'plaits' back from my shoulders. I made Janet do the same with her pyjama pants, but she wasn't much good at simpering. Janet preferred performing our special pig act, which involved making identical ugly pig faces at the mirror while swaying from side to side grunting. If my mum ever noticed us, she never said anything. She was too busy in her own dream world to worry about ours.

We had a younger sister named Cushla. Cushla was blond and blue eyed, and clever at getting her own way. Little 'Cushy', as we called her, hadn't yet realised what the world held in store for her with such a name. Cushy Rammsbottom; there was a certain smugness to be enjoyed in knowing that name would sort Cushla out and put the poor girl in her place when she started school. Blond hair and blue eyes would not be enough to keep her out of the outcast corner. Her place there was reserved.

2

Berry Street

If you venture a few miles north along Liverpool's Dock Road, you'll come to a place called Bootle. Bootle used to have its own hospital, town hall and public baths. It even had its own weekly newspaper called *The Bootle Herald*. We lived in Berry Street, and like most other streets in Bootle, the houses were terraced.

Among the rows of identical houses there was the occasional empty space, as conspicuous as a missing front tooth, where bombs had been dropped during the war. We lived next door to such a space. It was known by all as 'the debris'. My mum told us there had been a direct hit by a German bomber, that some old man had refused to get out of bed when the air-raid siren went and had been killed when a bomb dropped through his roof.

I used to spend hours on the debris, ferreting through the stones and bits of brick for a fragment of the unfortunate man's fossilised bones or teeth, as though he were the evolutionary missing link. His name was Mr Sanderson. My mum said she sometimes heard his ghost calling in the night; still calling for help. I kept listening in the night for Mr Sanderson's ghost, but there was so much of a living racket going on, especially on a Saturday night, a ghost couldn't get a look in. There were drunks singing, female voices shrieking and giggling, people congregating on the debris to argue or repeat their slurred goodnights and God blesses. The debris was used as a short cut from Berry Street through the back entries into the neighbouring Canal Street. The human noise became a background for sleep, as did the sound of the trains that rattled in and out of Bootle station every quarter of an hour, along the track running parallel to Berry Street.

Dogs wandered back and forth along the streets of Bootle just as people did. They loitered about the back entries where the bins were and, like people, they took short cuts across the debris. The high brick walls and outside lavatory roofs of the back yards was the realm of the cats. They sat serenely, as only cats can, watching the variety of people and dog life below. Sometimes in the dead of night a cats' concert would start up. Their child-like moaning would often wake us with a fright. They pierced the unconsciousness of sleep with their baleful, almost demonic crying. Then dogs from all over the neighbourhood would begin barking and howling their disapproval.

This nocturnal cacophony sounded like some wild orchestra warming up, playing in a strange key, just as certain types of Eastern music sound annoying to the untutored ear. It usually only lasted a couple of minutes before a loud human voice yelled the familiar 'Fuck off!' and threw something at the feline assembly on the lavatory roof. The man next door to us once threw a large family Bible from the attic window, which landed with a loud bang in our back yard. It scattered the screaming cats, and from that day on we referred to our neighbour as The Bible Basher, although he wasn't a bit religious.

The only other person I knew who made such use of large Bibles was our family doctor. She cured people's ganglions by bashing them to a pulp. Patients rarely ever needed any further treatment and seldom went back.

Sometimes local dogs, mostly medium-sized mongrels, roamed in packs; at other times they sat as individual guardians on their owner's front steps, signalling their territory by a throaty growl at anybody walking past. One particular dog looked like a mop minus the handle. Shaggy matted hair hung over his face, and as he sniffed along, nose to the ground, he looked like a mop cleaning the floor. He was always covered in muck and dust which clung to his shaggy tresses like dreadlocks. Almost everybody called him Mop-head, but his real name was Blackie.

When it came to naming their pets, Berry Street dog owners displayed a definite lack of imagination. There were four Blackies, a few Brownies and a couple of Goldies. To differentiate the dogs their surname was used, as with people. So if a dog lay dead in the gutter, people could say it was poor Blackie O'Flynn, as opposed to Blackie Milligan or Blackie Piper.

Most of the dogs were male. Female dogs tended to be put down as they were the cause of so much trouble. The Rainers across the road had a golden-coloured bitch named Goldie. When she went on heat about twenty dogs congregated outside the door, howling, peeing and scrapping for a good position in the queue. Mrs Rainer had one leg shorter than the other and tried chasing the love-sick mongrels with her crutch, but in the end there was nothing to be done but to have Goldie put down. Having dogs speyed or neutered was as unheard of as somebody going away skiing or sailing for a weekend.

In spite of the shortage of bitches, there was plenty of sexual activity among the dogs. It wasn't unusual to see three or four male dogs in the middle of the road, each mounting the other in a line, as though they were performing a circus act. When this happened, Mrs Milligan would come out with a bucket of cold water and throw it over the dogs, calling them dirty buggers. My mum laughed when she saw this and said 'needs must'. We all laughed.

The corner shop had a well-fed cream-coloured dog named Tim Harris. He was different from the others: not only did he have a proper dog name, but somewhere in his recent ancestry was solid labrador stock. Most of the day he sat on the step outside the shop allowing customers to step or trip over him and children to pat and poke his placid head. On warm summer days he would sit there panting with his tongue out, sporting a huge pink erection which poked out between his front paws. Inquisitive children from Berry Street and the neighbouring Canal Street spent many a Sunday afternoon studying the remarkable male anatomy of Tim Harris.

I loved dogs and never stopped pestering my parents for one, but the answer was always the same, we had a cat, and that was that. But in my imagination we had a beautiful black-and-tan Alsatian dog called Rover. I would take him for walks to the park, training him to sit and to stay. He was an obedient and faithful companion, scaring away lads when I gave the order to kill. Janet would spoil my reveries by pointing out that his name would have to be Rover Rammsbottom.

My mum was taciturn much of the time, but especially when my dad was around. She seemed to be shy of him. Maybe because he was fourteen years older. Their conversation seemed to dwell mainly on the weather or their bowel movements. People seemed to be keenly interested in bowel movements in those days. Perhaps it was a peculiar effect of the war years. My dad would come home from work, sit down at the table and start eating his tea. About half-way through his meal it wouldn't be unusual for him to ask,

'Have yer been to the lavvy today, Mammy?' He always called my mum 'Mammy' while we were there.

'No,' my mum would say, shaking her head and crinkling her nose. 'I didn't have any luck this mornin'.' To my mum, bowel movements were always a matter of luck. Nothing to do with diet or exercise, just luck – like the bingo.

One of the good things about my mum was that she hardly ever got angry, but when she did, everything about us was 'Bloody purgatory!' I always thought it was interesting how my parents referred to religion whenever they wanted to express a concern of some sort. 'Christ Almighty!' was the most common expression. I even heard my dad say, 'Lord love a duck' or just 'struth' when Janet broke a cup or committed some similar crime. Being a thoughtful type of person, I often wondered on the wording of such phrases. Lord love a duck. Why would anybody specifically request that Jesus love a duck? And which particular duck? It didn't make sense. But when, out of sincere curiosity, I asked my dad what he meant, I'd be threatened with a backhander and told not to cheek him, so I never found out.

Our parents referred to us so often as bitches I thought all females were bitches and males were buggers. When my parents spoke about the lads in the street, they called them hard-faced little buggers. Hearing these expressions repeated so frequently they became absorbed into the normal everyday vocabulary, so much so that I used them at school in blissful ignorance. During a lesson on opposite genders, I was scolded by the teacher for giving a reply which, to me, seemed the right and natural answer. We were asked what the opposite gender of a bitch was and I immediately came up with the answer – a bugger of course. Everybody in the class laughed and the teacher thought I was trying to be smart, but I wasn't.

Doreen Davy

My mum sang nearly all the time when my dad wasn't there. Some people thought she was cold-hearted because she was so detached and undemonstrative, but I knew she had plenty of feeling. It just wasn't directed towards her family. Something came over her when she was ironing. She always sang Irish rebel songs when she ironed. Her eyes misted over and her voice quivered with emotion for Kevin Barry, who gave his young life for the sake of liberty, or for the men and women who were hanged for the wearing of the green.

In spite of my young age I was moved by those songs, especially the one about Roddy McCorley marching to his fate on the bridge of Doon. Mother Ireland seemed always to be mourning her brave sons. From the words of the songs I could tell something cruel and unjust must have happened and people didn't want to forget. In my mum's case, it seemed to be like a ball of sorrow she carried inside her, preserved over the years and across the miles, only to be acknowledged when she ironed. Although she had lived most of her life in Liverpool, my mum had been born in Dublin and most of her family came from Ireland. She told me how her grandmother had been mutilated by the Black and Tans. They had cut her ear off for being out after curfew. The Black and Tans were horrible soldiers, she said, cruel bad buggers.

Some families have a bunch of flowers in the middle of their table; others might have a bowl of fruit or a salt and pepper set. We had none of these. Summer and winter, at the centre of our small oblong table sat half a raw onion. It sat there like a holy relic on a urine-coloured, cracked saucer. Every Friday my mum exchanged the old onion for a new one. Its function was to protect us from germs. My mum said our pet bird's longevity was proof of the germ-killing powers of the onion. His little birdcage hung directly over the table and he was supposed to be sixteen years old. In canary years that translates to two hundred years.

My mum also liked to sing when she worked in the kitchen peeling potatoes. Then it was arias from Italian operas. It should have been the other way round: the Irish songs with the potatoes, but for some reason, Irish ballads only went with the ironing.

She had always been a fan of Mario Lanza and had seen his film *The Great Caruso* many times. When she sang the famous melodies, she made the words up. As almost every word was via, la-la-la or mia, it seemed Italian must be a very easy language to learn. But I still couldn't work out what the songs were about.

One afternoon I stood in the doorway watching my mum in the kitchen. Her eyes were closed and she had one hand spread out across her chest. The other hand was waving the paring knife around. She was coming to the climax of the aria. On a final, prolonged 'mia' she brought the knife-wielding hand to rest on top of her other hand and her head fell forward dramatically. Then there was silence. Opening her eyes, she saw her small sole audience standing in the doorway. Without speaking she immediately resumed peeling the potatoes and launched into a brighter la-la-la song.

I asked her what the song had been about but she didn't like to be interrupted while she was singing. I was ignored. Later, I again asked about the sad knife song and she said it was about love. The love didn't seem to be anything to do with my dad, because as soon as he came home she clammed up. No singing, no talking other than answering his questions about the lavatory or agreeing that the evening sky looked like rain.

Most of the other women in the street bossed their husbands about, and in many ways it was a matriarchal neighbourhood. But for some reason my mum was the opposite. I think she could have been more companionable towards my dad but she chose to be subservient instead. Sometimes he tried to be playful, sneaking about on the floor while she was reading the newspaper, and mischievously pulling at one of the long fair hairs on her legs. She often wore her stockings rolled down to her ankles, a sight which seemed to make him frolicsome. I could tell from her expression that she hated it, but she said nothing. After tolerating a short time of him plucking at her legs she would stand up, put the newspaper down and silently return to the sanctity of the kitchen.

In spite of her strange, quiet ways I felt a great fondness for my mum. I wanted to be on her side, but I couldn't work out who the enemy was. She said our dad was a good man, a good father to us. He always gave her his wage packet every Friday night along with the occasional box of chocolates, so what was it that made her seem so aloof, so sad? To me, she was enigmatic, like an old burial tomb full of secrets.

Like Janet and me, my mum was tall and thin. Her hair was auburn and her skin was so white you could see the pale-blue spidery veins beneath the surface. Sometimes in her grey eyes there seemed to be a painful expression, of somebody wanting to embrace. But she hardly ever touched us, which is why I loved having nits. Then she had to touch me to de-nit my hair with the steel comb. It was heaven lying with my face in her onion-smelling lap having my hair examined. She would comb a few strands of wet hair through the small steel nit comb and then remove the catch into a scrap of newspaper. I must have been the only child at school who secretly enjoyed receiving a note from the dreaded Nitty Nurse.

Like most other women in the neighbourhood, my mum wore a wrap-around garment with big pockets known as a pinny, which made her look flat chested. She never wore a bra. Janet said she saw my mum putting her sagging tits in curlers every night before she went to bed. My mum laughed when she heard her saying that. We all laughed.

Not only did I feel alienated because of my embarrassing name; I didn't fit into any religious category either. People in our street were divided into two religions: Protestants, who tended to be in the Orange Lodge, and Roman Catholics. My mum had been brought up a Catholic, but was excommunicated when she married my dad, who was a Protestant. My dad referred to all religions, particularly the Roman Catholic religion, as 'a load of shite'. Janet and I went to a Protestant school.

One Sunday morning I discovered something extraordinary, something that had a great impact on me. I was waiting to be served in the corner shop when two girls I knew came in. They were dressed up as if for something special.

'Where are you goin' to?' I said.

'We're gettin' confirmed,' said Anne. 'We're Catholics.'

'What d'yer have to do?' I asked, enviously eyeing their dresses.

'We have to pick a new name for ourselves, after a saint,' answered Anne, blowing a small bubble of chewing gum in between chews.

'And I'm gonna be Veronica,' said the red-haired girl smoothing her dress sensuously with her freckly hand.

'Wharrabout you?' I asked Anne. I was becoming very interested.

'Bernadette,' said Anne with a slight preen and another bubble of chewing gum about to explode over her mouth. The woman behind the counter was shouting, 'Next,' but I'd forgotten what I was supposed to be buying. I looked at the two-shilling piece in my clammy hand but I still couldn't remember. I quickly left the shop and ran home.

As I entered our living room I suddenly recalled what it was I'd been sent to buy – a bottle of sterry. 'Sterry' was the word used for sterilised milk. 'They didn't have any left,' I lied to my mum, putting the money on the table. All I could think of was the new names – Veronica and Bernadette. Then, 'Mum, I wanna be a Catholic!' I announced in between breaths.

My mum didn't question why I should run back panting from the corner shop wanting to change my religion. 'How can I be one?' I persisted. I was used to her taking a long time before she answered anything.

'Go along to Saint Winny's next Sunday and see if they'll have yer,' came the reply. Saint Winnifred's was one of the many Catholic churches in the area, the closest one to Berry Street.

'Will yer come with me?' I asked, a pleading whine developing in my voice. 'Go on, come with me.'

'No,' she answered, the response accompanied by the usual shaking head and crinkling nose as she put the two-shilling coin back in her purse.

The thought of walking into the big Roman Catholic church known as Saint Winny's on my own was too frightening. My mum refused to accompany me, not because of any religious principle due to her excommunication; she just wasn't interested. I decided to try to make friends with a proper Catholic, so I'd have somebody to go with. Uncle Tommy (my mum's younger brother) was a Catholic, but I didn't like lads. Somebody like Anne Hayward would have to do.

So began my first spiritual quest: to become a Roman Catholic. The prospect of changing my Christian name was very exciting. I decided on 'Veronica' for my new name. People could call me 'Ronny' for short if they wanted. It sounded a bit cute, a bit

American, but it would create a new image. But then when I combined it with that other name, the result was a terrible alliteration. Ronny Rammsbottom! It was even worse than Deirdre. I'd have to be Bernadette instead.

At nine years old some urgent changes were needed in my life, and the sooner the better. Salvation awaited me in the Roman Catholic church.

3

To Be a Catholic

Every Friday evening Janet, Cushla and I each received a threepenny bit as pocket money. Normally we would dash to the corner shop and within minutes it would be spent on chocolate and lolly ices. But I'd decided to start saving mine. After a month I had the grand sum of one shilling and sixpence. This was made up of my own four threepenny bits and a sixpence I'd removed from my dad's overalls pocket. I hadn't meant to become a thief, but a plan had formed in my head which involved bribery. When obsessed with fanatical religious zeal, even theft must contribute to the grand cause.

One Sunday morning at about half-past eight, while my family was still in bed, I put on my red coat and walked quietly into the street. It was one of those beautiful mornings in October when a mild sea breeze was blowing from the Mersey and everything smelt fresh and exciting and sad all at the same time. The street was deserted and silent except for the far-away sound of a baby crying. On Sundays, most living things, young and old, seemed to sleep until mid-morning. I knew the Haywards would have to go to church so I hoped Anne might already be up.

Walking across the road, past the O'Flynns' house and the

Murrays' house, I felt overcome with pangs of guilt as I thought again of my plan. Being religious, Anne might reject my generous offer and ridicule me instead. But it was a case of nothing ventured, nothing gained. Even the houses seemed to be having a Sunday morning sleep-in along with their inhabitants. Curtains were drawn like tucked-in sheets. I felt like a trespasser, sneaking about with intent – which of course I was.

Standing outside Anne's house I observed the Hayward territory. It was similar to most of the other brick houses in the street. The step was newly scrubbed and there were red flowers in their tiny bit of garden at the front. The flowers looked like proper planted ones, not like the wild yellow peederbeds and buttercups that grew in our bit of grass. Their parlour window jutted out into the small garden. Dull green flakes of well-weathered paint still clung to the wooden window frame like tiny dried leaves.

Many families with lots of children slept downstairs as well as up, which was why the curtains in front parlours were drawn too. I could hear my own heart beating and wanted to run back home. This was an important mission. Four weeks of going without my three-pence worth of chocolate and making a thief of myself were now up for swaps.

The brave, more desperate part of me willed my hand to push the gate open and walk along the alien path. The door was made of thick brown wood with a big shiny knocker hanging from a brass lion's head. Standing on tip-toe I reached forward and banged the knocker. The loud, clear knocks on the door seemed to vibrate through the silent street. A curtain downstairs moved and bad-tempered footsteps tramped up the lobby. George Hayward opened the door just enough for his head to poke out. 'Wha' d'yer want?' he asked, looking at me through his black-rimmed glasses. His eyes were magnified through the thick lenses, which made him appear more manlike than boyish.

'Is Anne there?'

Before he could answer, a shrill female voice came from inside shouting, 'Who's that at this hour?'

'Some girl,' George called back to the voice.

There was now a female head at the parlour window and a hand pulling back the curtains. 'It's one of them Rammsbottom girls,' yelled the head. The sound of that name made me feel repulsed, like being hit with some slimy and offensive object. My body now obeyed all its natural instincts and I fled.

Back home everybody was still in bed. I looked at myself in the mirror over the Welsh dresser. It was starting to become a habit, this looking at myself in the mirror. My cheeks were flushed and my chin was quivering. Tiger, our grey-and-white cat, rubbed his body against my legs and miaowed for breakfast. He was a large, friendly moggy with a little pink neat nose and white whiskers.

Our other pet was Joey, the miraculous canary, who lived directly above the life-preserving onion on the table. The little bird lived out his long years in a small oval cage, which hung from the ceiling, resting against the window in the living room. At least he had a view of our backyard and could watch cats walking along the walls and the odd sparrow or pigeon flying about.

A malicious thought suddenly flashed across my mind. Tiger might like to eat Joey for breakfast. It was his natural intended sustenance, nature being red in tooth and claw. In their wild state cats hunted birds and mice to survive, although Tiger never seemed interested in hunting anything. He didn't have to. From one year to the next his breakfast, dinner and tea consisted of a couple of dollops of Kittycat plonked from a rusty spoon onto his saucer. A fresh meal of canary would make a nice change for him.

Climbing onto the table I came face to face with the little bird.

'The cat's hungry and wants to eat yer,' I whispered, my voice quivering. Joey looked at me with his head tilted to one side, the way some women do when they're asking a question, to show they're really interested. His eyes were like tiny brown beads, dull and lacking intelligence.

A pain was rising from my chest and heaving its way up to my throat. I could feel hot tears coming. Wanting to see the tears as well as feel them, I climbed down from the table and stood again before the mirror. Tears were rolling down my cheeks and my mouth was distorted into an ugly twitching shape, like a clown's. I watched myself wallowing in misery. After a while I wiped my messy face on the embroidered headrest of my dad's favourite armchair and gave Tiger his breakfast: two dollops of Kittycat.

Later on that Sunday morning, while Janet and I were playing with our dolls, there was a knock at the door. The next thing I knew, Anne Hayward was entering our living room. My mum had invited her in without warning. With the unexpected arrival of a guest I became suddenly aware that our house reeked of salt fish.

Every Sunday morning my dad was presented with a breakfast of boiled salt fish covered with melting butter, and a cup of tea on a tray. He never got out of bed on Sundays until after five o'clock in the evening, doing his 'Jimmy Riddles' in a po next to the bed. If Janet or I ever tried to watch, and we often did, he would tell us to fuck off, one hand pointing angrily towards the door. The other hand remained down by the po, holding onto something we were not allowed to know about. We were very curious.

'Was it you who called at our house before?' asked Anne looking down at our dolls.

'No,' I said. The lie came out before I had a chance to think.

'Mary said it was you, in a red coat,' continued Anne. 'She said she saw yer at the window.' I shook my head and continued dressing my doll in its blue woollen dress.

'Deirdre has got a red coat,' said Janet.

'D'yer wanna play dolls?' I asked, looking up at Anne as I nudged Janet with my elbow. Janet made a space for Anne to sit down with us, then we presented each of our dolls by name for Anne's inspection.

After a while, Anne invited us over to her house to meet her dolls. I told Janet she wasn't allowed to come as Anne was to play a major role in my plan and I wanted her all to myself. Janet trailed behind us anyway. Every time I looked behind, she'd look at the ground with a forced nonchalance, like a disobedient dog.

The inside of the Haywards' living room was like a miniature shrine. There were a couple of crucifixes on the wall and pictures of Mary holding baby Jesus. There was Mary alone looking upwards with a wistful expression and a picture of Jesus on his own with a similar expression. You could tell they were related. There was also a picture of an older man with a little white round hat and a white cloak. Anne said that he was called the Pope. On the sideboard there was more religious ornamentation: little knick-knacks, such as crosses, Jesus holding a lamb, Mary and her baby, and more pictures of halloed gentle faces with beautiful pale-blue eyes.

It was wonderful! My heart leaped with joy. What an aesthetically appealing religion: human forms that you could pray to, a gallery of saints who really existed behind the images. In our house there was nothing like this. Not a picture on the wall, not an ornament.

Anne's mother was sitting in an armchair reading a Sunday paper and sipping a cup of steaming tea. Two small children were climbing over each other on the floor, like a couple of playful puppies. Mrs Hayward looked up from her newspaper and said hello to me. She looked serene, like the pictures on the wall. Mr Hayward was just leaving. He was a short, dark-haired man dressed in a shiny suit, just off for a drink at the pub. Many people went straight from church to the pub. There were three pubs in Berry Street, each one well attended.

In the parlour, Anne showed me her two dolls, but I was more interested in the wooden crucifix over the bed. She slept in the parlour with three of her sisters. There were nine Hayward children living in the little two-bedroomed house. Some families in the street had twelve or more children living in a house. None of the houses had bathrooms – only an outside toilet.

Janet was still hanging about outside the Haywards' house. I poked my tongue out at her, but she remained defiant. She was pretending to admire the gate, making out she was examining the woodwork with a studious expression.

Later that afternoon, back at our house, the smell had changed from salt fish to roast dinner. Every week we had Sunday dinner at three o'clock. I told Anne to call back at about four o'clock, as I had something special to show her. The plan was now going well.

Janet, Cushla and I sat at the table eating a Sunday dinner of roast hearts, roast potatoes and boiled cabbage. The cabbage was always boiled until it was soggy, and grease from the meat was poured over the potatoes. It was superb. Janet and I stole the food from Cushla's plate while she wasn't looking. My mum ate her dinner on her own in the kitchen after taking my dad's plate up on a tray with a cup of tea and the *News of the World* for him to read. It was great having my dad in bed all day. We could come and go as we liked. My mum crept around the house so as not to disturb him.

Like a miser, I counted my money yet again. One shilling and sixpence. When Anne returned later, I showed her the small fortune. I said it could be hers if she would sell me her wooden crucifix, and if she would take me to Saint Winnifred's the following Sunday to ask the priest if I could become a Catholic. I explained how I'd like to change my name to Bernadette. She agreed to the deal.

At about a quarter past five, my dad finally got up. On Sundays he wore his dark grey trousers, usually with one brace hanging down over his hip, and a pair of old brown slippers. He put Brylcreem on his hair, even though he never went anywhere. It always marked the headrests on the armchairs, which quietly annoyed my mum. Cushla was sitting on his knee playing with one of his braces, pulling it out as far as she could and then letting it go with a ping. She was his favourite.

For our tea we were having salmon paste sandwiches and chocolate cake. The cake was from Sayers' cake shop. We ate in silence except for the chomping and swallowing of food. When my mum cut the cake into six pieces, there was an extra piece left over. Every Sunday she cut the cake this way and every Sunday it caused trouble. As of right, Cushla was given the spare piece of cake. My mum said it was to fatten up her spindly legs. As usual Janet and I complained about the unfairness of Cushla getting the extra piece. My dad called us peevish bloody bitches and banged the table with his fist. We enjoyed working him up to this state, but it was important to know how far to go. Complaining past the safety limits could turn dangerous.

Our complaining always took the form of a whining, repetitive muttering sound, usually reaching a crescendo when Cushla's greedy outstretched hand was about to make contact with the cake. My dad immediately stood over us with his fist ready to strike. It was wiser to keep our heads down and say nothing as the troublesome slice settled on Cushla's plate. Our little sister beamed in triumph, her expression gloating, daring us to continue moaning. Sometimes my dad's threatening stance made us giggle uncontrollably as we cowered, and we would end up getting a hard backhander across the head. Then the laughter would turn to crying. Even at the tender age of four there was a gleam of delight in Cushla's eyes when this happened. She enjoyed the power of the cake.

After tea my dad went outside to the lavatory. He never spent less than twenty minutes there. Seizing the chance, I ran across to Anne's house. This time I was not afraid of their well-scrubbed doorstep or intimidated by the big door knocker. I had only twenty minutes in which to conduct the business deal, so within sixty seconds I was standing in the Haywards' lobby, calling out like a cheeky gypsy selling pegs.

That evening the wooden crucifix hung on the wall in our bedroom, precariously stuck to the wallpaper with strips of Sellotape. I had given Anne a shilling for it and she was to receive the remaining sixpence after she had taken me to church. Our house had two bedrooms upstairs. Janet and I shared a double bed in one room; Cushla slept in a single bed in our parents' larger room.

Practising the sign of the cross with my hand, I knelt on the bed before the crucifix. The gaunt body of Jesus was hanging on the cross complete with crown of thorns, a loincloth, and nails in his hands and feet. His presence made me feel part of something much larger. I now felt I belonged, like being a member of a special club. Janet said she didn't like it in our room. I told her she would be safe from now on, as Jesus would watch over us, and besides, I was going to be a Catholic so she had better get used to it.

That night, while we were asleep, the crucifix fell down from the wall and hit Janet on the head, cutting her just above an eyebrow. 'Serves yer right for sayin' yer don't like it,' I said, wiping her bloody forehead with my hanky. She looked sulkily at the cross, finally realising the power of Jesus.

'Will you bitches put that bloody light out!' came the familiar voice from the next room. After a whispered goodnight, and amen to Jesus, I put Him under my pillow and went back to sleep.

After school the next day I went across to Anne's house. She told me she could get me more crucifixes or pictures if I wanted them. She showed me a beautiful gold-framed picture of a halloed woman who was dressed like a nun in a pale-blue robe. Her opened palms were facing up, and her expression was even more serene than the others. Anne told me this was Saint Bernadette, who had experienced a vision of Our Lady. Saint Bernadette. My new name. My own special saint.

'How much?' I asked.

Anne studied the picture from various angles. 'Two bob.'

'Two bob!' That would take me eight weeks to save.

'It's a real gold frame yer know,' said Anne, passing it to me for a closer examination.

Two shillings was a lot of money, but I was determined to have it. I agreed to the price and Anne said she'd hold it for me until I saved the amount. Her brother George had overheard our discussion and asked me if I'd like to buy his Saint Christopher for a shilling. 'Maybe,' I said, studying the grubby looking thing around his neck. Business in the Haywards' house was booming.

Janet had a plaster across her forehead where the cross had

scratched her when it fell. My mum said I had to put the crucifix somewhere else, not above the bed anymore. I Sellotaped it to the opposite wall so I could lie in bed looking at it, and if it fell down again, it would land on the chest of drawers.

Two shillings? Where would I get two shillings without having to save it from my threepence a week? I looked down the sides of the couch, always a good place for finding coins, but I only managed to find a couple of buttons, a match and a few peanuts.

'Wharra yer lookin' for?' asked Janet, ever inquisitive.

'Nothin'. I'm just lookin' under the couch, that's all,' I explained.

'I know where there's some money,' said Janet.

'Where?'

'Down at the bus station.' The bus terminal was through the subway under the railway. The number 61 and 49 buses stopped there to change drivers and conductors.

'What d'yer mean?' I asked, quietly admiring Janet's hidden wealth of knowledge.

Janet explained that somebody in her class had told her that the dockers coming home on a Friday night often dropped money onto the floor of the bus when they fumbled about to pay their fares. They always had a few drinks before coming home on Fridays and were not very alert to what was falling from their pockets.

A feeling of elation filled me as I imagined the Friday night buses knee-deep in silver coins. It could only be the work of the Lord. Janet agreed to come with me to the bus station the following Friday evening. The only trouble was my dad didn't allow us to go out while he was around, so it would have to be when he went to the lavatory after his tea.

That night I prayed to the wall. 'Dear Jesus, please could you arrange for our father, Mr Harold Rammsbottom, to spend longer than usual in the lavatory this Friday evening.' I also asked for a good find of coins on the bus floor. Jesus just kept His eyes closed, His head slumping motionlessly to one side. But I knew He could hear me.

Faith – I had it in abundance. I fell asleep in the certainty that my prayers were as good as answered.

4

A Pair of Lying Bitches

There was always a happy, end-of-the-week feeling on a Friday evening. It was my favourite time of the week. People in the chippy seemed more friendly with each other; they had money in their pockets and there were chips in the fryer. I loved watching the two women who worked in the chippy dexterously wrapping the newspapers around the hot bundles, their sleeves rolled up to their elbows, both of them calling every customer 'luv'.

I raced to the top of Coffee House Bridge carrying the fish and chips for our tea that evening. Too excited to walk, I could only gallop like a wild horse, holding the greasy hot parcel under my arm. The sky was grey, reflecting the monochromatic streets and canal below it. Standing on my tiptoes at the top of Coffee House Bridge I could see the docks in the distance. I could also hear the clatter of Bootle, like an urban heartbeat. The faraway squeals of a thousand kids and the distant rumble of buses and lorries along Stanley Road. The Southport-to-Liverpool train creaked wearily along, while the sounds of cranes from the docks reminded me of my dad, who was working somewhere down there among it all.

All the sights and sounds together created a special feeling of familiarity and security. I pressed the hot parcel of chips against my body. The smell was mouth watering and I made a little hole in the paper near the top, pulling a few salt-and-vinegared steaming chips out to eat on the way home.

I would often stop on the bridge and look down into the murky water of the Leeds-to-Liverpool canal. My mum said it was full of dead dogs and cats and diphtheria. I would think about little Christy Murphy, who had drowned there a few months earlier, imagining what it must have been like for him. He was only four (the same age as Cushla) when he decided to go fishing one Sunday morning while everybody was asleep. He had dug up a worm, tied it onto the end of a long piece of white sewing cotton and tied the cotton to a bamboo stick. They found his makeshift fishing rod on the bank, and Christy's body floating, face down, under the bridge. Everybody knew there weren't any fish in the canal, but nobody told Christy.

Sometimes I climbed down to the gravelly bank and listened for Christy's little ghost calling. I never heard it. I wasn't very good at hearing ghosts, not like my mum was.

For tea that evening, along with the fish and chips, we had buttered bread and a delicacy known as soggy peas. Soggy peas were lovely, even nicer than the chips. I always made a chip butty with my few remaining chips. The taste of hot chips against the melting butter and soft white bread was delicious.

It was five to five, the twilight time when all the men of the neighbourhood began to reappear. Janet and I waited for my dad to materialise at the top of Berry Street. He always travelled to work and back on his bike. Most of the men did. They all wore a type of uniform consisting of a flat cap on their heads and bicycle clips around their trouser bottoms. If it was cold my dad wore a heavy, navy-blue jacket with silver buttons, which gave him a slightly naval appearance. For the milder weather he wore a light-blue denim jacket.

Sometimes on a Friday he would have a brown paper parcel under one of his arms. It would be a bag of chocolates from Woolworths. If we caught sight of the bag, we would run up to his bike before it reached our house and almost attack him in a frenzy of excitement and greed. But this particular Friday evening there wasn't any parcel under his arm, so we went back inside the house with sullen faces. No chocolate, no greeting.

I watched carefully as my dad ate his tea. My mum was still in the kitchen and he was calling to her with his mouth full of chips, asking her the usual question – had she managed to move her bowels that day? She appeared for a few seconds around the door to shake her head and say she'd had a bit of luck, but not much. From the clock on the mantelpiece I could see it was already twenty past five. I knew that a couple of buses were due in at the station at half past. I wished he would hurry up.

He continued eating his tea, looking up at the sky through the net curtains, probably preparing his next comment to Mammy about it looking like rain tonight. But the comment wasn't made. Instead he lifted one buttock to allow a fart to escape. That was a good sign. I was wishing so much that he'd hurry up and go to the toilet I was holding my breath. I'd already made sure he had plenty of newspapers in there, small bits for wiping and big bits for reading. I'd even put a picture of a woman in a bikini on top of the cistern (in the reading category), because I knew he liked to spend time studying such things. I'd noticed him when he was reading the *News of the World* or *The People*, he would just stare for ages at those sorts of pictures and then turn the page over quickly if my mum came into the room.

At last he stood up and took his usual couple of Woodbines and a box of matches. 'Off to the lavvy for a smoke, Mammy,' he said, opening the back door and heading down the backyard. I watched him through the net curtains. Shuffling along in his overalls, his body seemed weary with the routine of it all. As he opened the crooked green door to the lavatory Janet and I bolted out through the front door.

When we arrived at the bus station a number 61 was just pulling in. It was packed with men in flat caps scrambling to get off. The driver and conductor disappeared into the little mobile canteen which was permanently positioned in the terminus. Janet was to look downstairs while I checked upstairs. The bus stank, mainly of tobacco smoke and beery breath. I decided to start at the front and work my way back. There were plenty of cigarette butts, empty matchboxes and bits of paper on the floor. There was even a gob of yellow phlegm, which made me feel slightly repulsed.

I was half-way through my disgusting task and hadn't found anything. Then I saw it. A large silver coin lying by itself, a half-crown. A miracle! Two shillings and sixpence! Thanking Jesus, I slowly picked the coin up and lifted it to my nose. I wanted to smell something that had been sent from heaven. But there was nothing divine about the smell. It had the usual mucky tobacco-money smell of men's hands. My mum said you should never put money in your mouth because a Chinaman might have touched it. I knew from the pictures in Anne Hayward's house that Jesus had blue eyes, so he couldn't have been an Asian.

I quickly kissed the coin and put it in my pocket, continuing my search down towards the back of the bus. Maybe I could buy the Saint Christopher too. Suddenly a man's voice rang out. 'What the fuckin' hell are you up to then?'

A bus conductor was at the top of the stairs. He was looking at me groping around on my hands and knees. I wanted to say I was

A Dandelion By Any Other Name

praying, but I said nothing. Standing up, I walked towards the stairs, wanting to get off the bus and run home with my half-crown.

'What's your name then?' he asked, not moving out of the way to let me pass.

'Bernadette,' I said, liking the sound of it.

'Well, Bernadette, I know what you're up to. You're looking for money aren't yer?'

I nodded. He was looking at me the same way teachers do before they cane you. Pretending to be sorry but really enjoying it.

'And have yer found any?'

'No, nothin',' I lied.

'How old are yer?' he asked, putting his hand on my shoulder. I didn't answer. I started to worry that his hand might wander further down my body. Into my pockets. I continued looking down the stairs, not saying anything as his hand massaged my shoulder.

After a few seconds he removed his hand and moved out of the way. He then followed me down the stairs. Janet was standing outside sucking her thumb the way she usually did when she was anxious. The conductor leaned down into our faces. His skin was poxy, like an old dart board, and his breath smelt of tobacco and rotten teeth.

'If yer ever wanna look for money, yer come and ask me first. D'yer understand?' We both nodded meekly.

Just as another bus pulled in we headed back through the subway towards Berry Street. I touched the half-crown in my pocket and pressed it into my palm. 'There was a sixpence under the back seat but the man stopped me pickin' it up,' said Janet, her voice verging on tears.

I opened my sweaty palm triumphantly, revealing the half-crown I had found.

'Wow!' said Janet looking behind us to check nobody was following. 'What'll we buy on it?'

'You can have a frozen Jubilee and a lolly pop, but I'm savin' the rest,' I whispered. 'And you've not to say anything to dad.' Even though the promised items were only worth about fourpence, she agreed.

We ran back home. Luckily my dad was still in the toilet. I sprinted upstairs and closed the bedroom door. Kneeling before the cross, I heard the toilet being flushed at the end of the yard. I thanked Jesus profusely for all His help.

The next day, Saturday, the beautiful picture of Saint Bernadette was on my little table next to the bed. I asked my mum to come and see it. She looked at it without saying anything. 'Don't yer like it Mum?' I asked. 'It's real gold.' She looked at the cross on the wall and back again at the picture. The right side of her mouth curled up in its familiar way, which always crinkled her right nostril. This negative expression was accompanied by a slow shaking of her head which could only be interpreted as no.

'Don't you believe in heaven and hell?' I asked.

'Hell's on earth,' she replied with unusual promptness.

'What about when yer die, when yer go to heaven?' I asked. I knew from the hymns we sang in assembly at school that heaven awaits the good. My favourite hymn was 'Love Divine'. I loved its words just as much as the tune.

But my mum didn't seem too interested in going to heaven. She looked out the bedroom window, gently moving one half of the net curtain to make it even with the other. She sighed wearily before explaining that people only believed in heaven for comfort, and that all religions were made up – for comfort. She said nobody knows what happens to people when they die, and nobody had ever been back to tell.

'What about Mr Sanderson's ghost?' I asked. My mum was a strange combination of superstition and cynicism. She looked at me with pursed lips and walked as silently as a nun out of the room, gently closing the door behind her. No wonder she'd been excommunicated, I thought. It was hard to credit somebody not liking Jesus or the beautiful Saint Bernadette.

Cushla had sneaked in while my mum was in the bedroom and had not sneaked out again. Normally I didn't allow her in our room as she was clumsy with things. I told her Saint Bernadette could perform miracles, that she had seen a vision of Our Lady in a waterfall. Cushla looked at the picture and reached a small meddlesome hand out to touch it.

'No, you're only allowed to look, not to touch,' I told her. 'It's real gold and worth a lot of money.'

There was now a bowl of holy water on the dressing table. I had blessed it myself. It had 'HOLY WATER' written on the side of the bowl in purple crayon. Dipping my fingers, I chanted 'domino domini' as I flicked the holy drips at Cushla's face. She immediately retaliated by calling me a dickarse and left the room with a sulking pout.

Sitting alone before the dressing-table mirror, I placed a white-and-blue teatowel across my head. I stretched out my hands, palms facing upwards and looked at myself in the oval-shaped glass. I stared until my vision was out of focus. You're supposed to see the Devil if you stare long enough in a mirror. For a couple of seconds I looked just like her, Saint Bernadette. My eyes suddenly refocused and I saw my own intense face looking back at me. Tomorrow I was to accompany Anne to Saint Winifred's church, where I'd become a Roman Catholic, and from then on be known simply as Bernadette. I took the teatowel off my head and went downstairs. I told my mum I'd just experienced my first holy vision. She never questioned it for a moment.

Sunday morning, I lay in bed sulking. My legs were still smarting from the strapping I'd received the night before. All hopes for a new religion, a new name and a new life lay in ruins. Instead I had been called all manner of loathsome names: a bitch, a thief, a liar and a little slut. I particularly didn't like that last insult. Women called Brenda Rainer (a girl who lived across the road) a little slut. The dictionary said it was a dirty, untidy female. Brenda Rainer never looked dirty or untidy to me. People always used horrible names for females they didn't like: scrubber, slut, hussy, scutty, cunt. There must be something about the 'u' sound. Like the word fuck. I used to think it was only used in Liverpool, but when television took over I was surprised when I heard it spoken with an American accent. The way he said it, it sounded almost posh, pretentious. It had no bite to it. With a Liverpudlian accent the word was jagged and emphatic, the upper teeth bared, biting into the lower lip like an animal ready to attack, the whole face thrust forward to shoot the word out like a poisoned dart. That was a real 'fuck'.

Cushla had snitched on me. She told my dad about the religious goings on in my bedroom. I never knew he was such a fanatical Protestant. He protested wildly. When he came into the room and saw my little holy shrine he started cursing under his breath and turned on the light to get a better look. What he saw before him manifested itself in the most ludicrous of expressions. He yelled out 'flamin' arseholes!' Those two words conjured up such a bizarre image in my mind that an urge to giggle rose inside me, but was quickly suppressed. He told me to get that Catholic shite out of the house.

I looked at Jesus on the cross but He didn't move. I was half expecting my dad to be struck dead for saying such a thing, but he just continued tut-tutting and blowing air through his pursed lips as he left the room. He always seemed to feel awkward in our bedroom, as though he were trespassing and needed to get out quickly.

As I was taking the cross down from the wall, there was a commotion downstairs. A woman's voice was shouting. There were always women's voices shouting in Berry Street, but this one seemed to be shouting into our lobby and my dad's voice was shouting back. Then footsteps and voices were coming up the stairs. The door of my bedroom swung violently open as my dad entered again, followed by Mrs Hayward and Anne, then by my mum, Janet and Cushla.

'That's the one!' yelled Mrs Hayward pointing to Saint Bernadette, 'our family heirloom, pinched by your girl here.'

My dad picked up the picture and shoved it into Mrs Hayward's arms.

'And that belongs to us as well,' she said, looking at the crucifix I was holding. It had Sellotape and torn bits of wallpaper attached to the Lord's feet, arms and head. My dad snatched the cross from me. 'Here, take the bloody things back where they belong,' he said, pointing the crucifix at her as though it were a sword. Anne took it from him and quickly turned to leave the room.

'But I paid for them,' I whined. 'I gave Anne money for them. Two bob for the picture and a shillin' for the cross.' Nobody seemed to take any notice of my explanation. Mrs Hayward bundled Anne and her sacred ornaments down the stairs. My dad followed them to the front door, cursing.

I wanted my mum to help me, but she just stood there wrapped in her silence, looking through me rather than at me. Cushla was peeping out from behind my mum, holding onto her pinny for protection and sucking a thumb. Janet sat on the bed next to me. She, too, was sucking her thumb.

'I did pay for them,' I cried. 'They were mine, weren't they Janet?' Janet nodded shyly, reluctantly confirming the statement.

A thudding of slippered feet was coming back up the stairs. Janet began to cry. My dad's whiskery grey face blazed at me. 'Did you steal them bloody things?'

'No, I paid out three bob for them.'

He didn't look convinced. 'You bloody well pinched them, didn't yer?'

'I didn't! I already told yer, I paid three bob to Anne for them. She's the one who's stealin'.'

'And where the hell did yer get that sort of money, eh?'

'I found it.'

'Don't you lie to me, yer little bitch.' His arm was held up ready to lash out one of his backhanders.

'She did find it,' sobbed Janet. This fresh evidence caused an interval of a few seconds' silence while my dad reviewed the situation.

'You're nothin' but a pair of lyin' bloody bitches!'

'Down at the bus station,' cried Janet. 'That's where she found it.'

My dad looked at my mum as though an explanation was in order, but she said nothing. 'The fuckin' bus station! Yer got that money down at the fuckin' bus station?' His words were exploding out of his mouth with spittle.

'Yes!' I shouted back. 'The busman let me look on the floor for money and I found half a crown.'

A Dandelion By Any Other Name

My dad's hands were now in an unco-ordinated frenzy trying to unfasten his belt. I knew what was coming next. 'You little slut!' he shouted as the belt whipped against my bare legs. Janet buried her face in her hands as I continued screaming and squirming to get away from the hard, leathery lashes. All the time he was calling me horrible names and said he would kill me if I ever went near the bus station again. My mum finally intervened and called out for him to stop strapping me, but not until my legs were red with stripes.

He finally stopped and flung his belt over his shoulder the way hunters do with dead things. I heard him almost slip on the steps as he shuffled angrily back down the stairs. My mum took my shoes off and I got into bed without getting undressed. I was still crying as they all quietly left the room and my mum turned the light off. It was about half-past five in the evening, half-way between light and dark, half-way between cold and warm. I could hear kids still playing in the street. The outside world sounded as though everybody was enjoying themselves, while I was left alone feeling unjustly blamed and cruelly beaten. Jesus had allowed something very unfair to happen. He had watched and done nothing.

I felt in need of some comfort. Anything would do, even magic, or voodoo, or aliens from outer space. Anything that might provide a bit of spiritual solace. I wondered about life and why I had been born with such a horrible name, and why my dad should prefer to believe strangers, Catholics at that, rather than his own daughter.

The evening shadows were beginning to transform the bedroom furniture into the familiar night creatures. The box on top of the wardrobe turned into a monkey. I watched it gradually change from a harmless cardboard box into a wild, malicious monkey, showing its teeth in a snarl as though it were trying to say fuck off. Every night it came to sit on top of the wardrobe. It didn't do anything, it just stared at me with its hostile expression. I put my head under the blankets and eventually fell asleep curled up as small as I could.

5

To Be a Protestant

My dad had strange ways of saying he was sorry. On Sunday evening I was still sulking from the previous night's hiding. He asked me if I'd like to play Heads or Tails with his copper coins, the pennies and halfpennies. It wasn't very often he played that game with us, so I guessed he must have been feeling sorry for me. He let me call. If I won, I could keep it. I kept losing, but he let me keep them anyway. I played in silence, my lips pursed, my eyes looking down so as not to see his face; I was not going to be jollied out of a legitimate sullenness for a few pennies.

When the time came for the Sunday evening cake to be cut into six, he suggested that Cushla give me half of the extra piece. Of course this immediately started Janet grumbling about unfairness and Cushla whining that the whole extra piece of cake belonged to her as of right – 'Wharrabout me spindly legs?' – and she shouldn't have to share it. My dad's temper flared up immediately, calling us all bloody peevish bitches of hell. As he stood up, he kicked the chair in anger, grabbed his cigarettes and matches, and amidst a cacophony of cursing, banging and farting, he shuffled down the back yard in retreat towards the lavatory.

With my dad out of the way the cake was literally up for grabs.

Janet and I tore at it like animals while Cushla's body turned rigid with anger. She banged her plate and threw it across the table knocking the precious onion off its saucer. Then she noticed my dad's piece of cake sitting on its own, unclaimed. But Janet saw it too. As Cushla reached out, Janet had the cake secured, guiding it towards her own open mouth. Cushla was not having a good day. Feeling the injustice of it all, she screamed obscenities and squirmed in anger on the floor.

My mum looked as though a life sentence had just been passed on her as she watched Janet and me laughing and encouraging Cushla's tantrum. We loved our little sister throwing tantrums. It was great entertainment. For a four-year-old she had a vicious temper. My mum took her own cake and sandwich into the kitchen and quietly closed the door behind her.

I never spoke to Anne Hayward again. If we met in the shop or the street we didn't acknowledge each other. My quest to become a Catholic had been short lived. There was no option but to remain Deirdre Rammsbottom (with three M's) until I was a bit older, then I would marry anybody who might want me.

A few weeks after the crucifix trouble, another Berry Street child was killed. Anne's little sister Tracey was run over by the ice-cream van outside their house. She was two years old and had managed to crawl under the van while it stopped to serve ice-cream. The van was chiming 'The Happy Wanderer' as its back wheel rolled over Tracey's blond head. She died in Walton Hospital three hours later.

The following summer I somehow managed to make friends with Brenda Rainer, the slut from across the road. She was about a year older than me, but mentally and physically she was years ahead. My mum said Brenda was sex mad, that she leered at men with a hungry look. Even on the school photograph, my mum said she was leering at the photographer. I could see what she meant. Brenda's head was bent forward almost onto her chest, with eyes looking straight ahead and mouth half smiling. Yes, she certainly looked sex mad and leering. I practised a leer in the mirror, but I couldn't manage that special look.

The Rainers had recently acquired a new puppy, which was the reason I came to make friends with Brenda in the first place. His name was Billy (after King Billy of Orange), and he was a beautiful little black-and-tan mongrel. They were staunch members of the Orange Lodge and took their enthusiasm to great lengths. Only orange marigolds grew in their little front garden: I suspected they resented the grass being the colour green, the Catholic colour, but there wasn't much they could do about that. Their door and windowsills were painted orange and over the fireplace hung a huge portrait of King Billy on an undersized horse. Being such fervent Protestants they had a low regard for Catholics, although they were surrounded by them in Berry Street.

Mr Rainer was a tall man in his fifties. He had big bushy eyebrows under which small blue eyes darted about like a pair of moths. His hair grew out rather than down, all bushy and white like a mad professor's, but he wasn't very clever. My mum said some of the women in the street called him a MaryAnne. The only thing I admired about him was his ability to play the accordion. He could play most tunes by ear, not needing any sheet music. Mostly he played Orange Lodge songs such as 'The Battle of the Boyne'.

Mrs Rainer was a cripple. She could get around by jutting one hip out in front of her and, with the aid of a walking stick, bring the rest of her body forward in a sort of semicircle. Watching her get about was a bit like watching a yacht sailing to windward. She was a very plain woman with a sallow complexion and a mean mouth.

One sunny afternoon when I should have been at school, I was sitting on our front step in a patch of sun watching Pat Gawler. The Gawlers lived next door but one to us. They were Catholics and Pat was the eldest daughter. She was about fifteen but had the build of a hefty forty-year-old. She didn't work, nor did she go to school. She seemed to spend much of her day on duty at the front gate, watching. Pat's mother, Mrs Gawler, would come out to take over the watch while Pat went inside, probably for a teabreak. They were both very piglike and it didn't take much effort to imagine them both as characters from a Beatrix Potter story, up on their hind legs dressed in flowery aprons, their sleeves rolled up displaying fat little trotters as they leaned on the gate. I never discovered what the Gawlers were on guard against, what they were watching out for. A German invasion?

Pat had her hand over her eyes, shading them from the sun as she peered up and down the road. Everything was quiet and still on the Western Front. Then Pat noticed something moving. It was Mrs Rainer from across the road. Pat's great body immediately went into alert mode as though the enemy had been sighted. She grunted the information back to her mother, who came bustling out to the gate. Mrs Gawler put one hand to her brow, the other on her hip, while Pat pointed a finger in the direction of the Rainers' house.

Across the road Mrs Rainer had one hand over her brow, the other on her stick. She stared defiantly back at the Gawlers. I crept forward to get a better viewing position for the battle that was about to commence. High Noon had come to Berry Street. For a few seconds there was a menacing silence, while both sides contemplated their strategies. Mrs Gawler fired the first shot.

'Wha' the fuckinell are you lookin' at?'

'I wouldn't fuckin' know,' came the immediate reply from across the road.

My mum must have heard the argument starting and came out to make sure I wasn't caught in the crossfire. The battle continued in the same manner.

'Wha' did you fuckin' well say?'

'You fuckin' well heard.'

As my mum steered me inside, the quarrel between the two naturally turned to religion with the Gawlers being called Catholic shite. In retaliation the two porcine women started yelling abuse about Protestant bastards. I only managed to hear a few more words before my mum closed the door and directed me into the living room. 'Yer don't wanna listen to all that,' she said.

But I did. I did.

The Rainers seemed to live in a time warp (around 1690) when King William of Orange beat the Catholics in Ireland at the Battle of the Boyne. For some reason they kept it going as though it were something glorious and relevant to modern times. When I brought my dolls over to show Brenda (who wasn't a bit interested in playing dolls), Mrs Rainer was alarmed to hear that one of my dolls was called Mary. 'A horrible Catholic name!' she said.

Mary quickly became Linda.

It was the beginning of July and the Rainers were preparing for their big day on the 12th. On that day every year, the Lodge marched. The Rainers belonged to the Bank Hill Orange Lodge. They usually spent a day at Southport and marched back through the streets – a procession of pipe bands, banners, girls dressed in long orange dresses, and, of course, King Billy with his queen.

Brenda showed me her full-length orange satin dress. That

alone was enough to make me desperately want to join the Lodge. As I wasn't allowed to dress up in white along with the Catholic girls, surely I would find something glamorous to wear by joining the Lodge. After all, officially I was a Protestant. I asked Mr and Mrs Rainer if I could join. They weren't very happy about my mother being a Catholic, but they said they'd see what the higher officials thought and would let me know.

I didn't bother telling my parents. While my dad was in bed most Saturdays and Sundays, I went across to Brenda's house. My mum didn't know where I was going, and she didn't ask.

Brenda always seemed to have money and was very generous. If she went to the corner shop to buy herself an ice-cream or chocolates, she always bought me whatever she was having. I noticed some women in the shop looking at Brenda and signalling to each other. Their eyes looked her up and down with an expression of disgust. I'd noticed this type of female warfare before. Brenda must have become inured to it, because she took absolutely no notice of them. They probably called her a slut when we left, but to me she was a good friend. And I was getting lots of free ice-creams.

One wet Sunday afternoon I was sitting in the Rainers' living room. Brenda and I were trying to teach Billy how to sit. Mr Rainer was in the front parlour playing his accordion and the sound of the lively music charmed me. Hovering outside the parlour doorway, I quietly observed him. He was standing with the accordion strapped over his shoulders, swaying about to the music. He once told me that a good Orangeman plays on, even if his head has been chopped off. I tried to imagine him playing and dancing without a head, but his bushy eyebrows were going up and down to the music, like a kind of metronome, which tended to spoil the decapitation concept.

A Dandelion By Any Other Name

I'd only been watching him for about a minute when Brenda pulled me back into the living room. She had that leering look about her, the look that had been captured on the school photograph. I wanted to go back into the parlour to watch her father, but she asked me to kneel on the mat in front of the armchair. The next thing I knew, she had taken her knickers off and was squatting on the armchair with her knees apart. Her fingers were busy playing a different piece of music. She was totally uninhibited and didn't seem too worried about her father coming in.

'It feels nice,' she said as the puppy clumsily attempted to climb onto the chair, his tail wagging and his nose sniffing about. 'Why don't you put your mouth there?' she asked, pointing to the area where her fingers were busy.

I told her I didn't want to, although the dog was certainly showing some interest. I kept looking at the door, worrying about Mr Rainer appearing. He had started playing a slower tune – 'Cruising Down the River'.

'Use yer fingers then,' Brenda ordered, pulling at my hand and placing it where hers had been. Her body squirmed on the chair while my fingers acquiesced to her demands. The accordion seemed to become louder, and increased in tempo. Suddenly the door opened and the music burst into the room. I pulled my hand away, but Brenda didn't move.

'Go on, lovey,' said Mr Rainer, as he swayed about the room, 'just carry on with your game.'

Brenda seized my hand back and I reluctantly continued with what I knew was unacceptable behaviour, certainly not the sort of thing you did in front of grown-ups. Mr Rainer now swayed about like a drunken man, playing his accordion in a frenzied manner. All the while his little blue eyes looked down at us as he nodded and smiled his approval. Brenda now had her head back and was breathing heavily. They both frightened me.

I stood up and ran from their house as fast as I could. I never told anybody about the games the Rainers played on a Sunday afternoon.

The next day Brenda informed me that I wasn't allowed to join the Orange Lodge because my mother was a Catholic. It seemed there was no opportunity at all for me to dress up and be someone special. Neither Catholics nor the Protestants wanted me in their clubs. So at the age of ten, my main goal in life was to get married. Not only would I get to wear a beautiful long dress, but I would be able to change my jinx-ridden name forever.

On the 12th of July the pipes and drums could be heard as the Lodge members prepared to board the train for Southport. On their return they were to march from Litherland Station to Bootle Town Hall. They usually marched along Stanley Road, past Marsh Lane, where all the Catholics gathered for a fight, and then down Merton Road. I'd never been allowed to witness that exciting event, but I decided this year I would. I told my mum I was going to Marsh Lane to see the Lodge march past on their way home.

'Yer dad'll go mad,' she said.

'I don't care,' I answered. 'I wanna see them.'

All day I watched the clock in the living room. Its hands moving slowly through the minutes and hours. It was another one of those days when I should have been at school. At half-past four I told my mum I was going to play with Pauline from school, that she'd invited me to her house. My mum knew I was lying, but she just looked at me with her negative expression and said I'd end up getting hurt if I went to Marsh Lane. When I got there people were already starting to line the pavement to watch the parade. Some had bags of half-rotten tomatoes. One man was showing another some eggs he had in his pocket. I walked towards Litherland so I could march back some of the way with the parade before it reached the notorious Marsh Lane.

Soon, the drums and pipes could be heard in the distance. It was a very exciting sound and I wormed my way to the front of the crowd to get a good view. Around the corner came the flying banners of the Bank Hill Orange Lodge. Rows of men wearing black bowler hats and orange sashes marched along the road. As they marched they sang a song about the Battle of the Boyne: 'And they fought for the glorious King William, On the green grassy banks of the Boyne.'

They also sang another song with a catchy little tune but provocative words:

Bobby, bobby don't take me,
take that feller behind the tree,
he belongs to Pope Parrie,
and I belong to King Billy.
Eee, iye, Paddy was a bastard,
Paddy was a bastard all his life.

The leader of the band was a great bulk of a man with a handlebar moustache and a big baton. He quivered with importance as he twirled the baton in the air, doing elaborate juggling tricks in an ecstasy of movement. Behind him came another enormous man with a huge drum. He wore some sort of animal skin over his front, from a tiger or a leopard, and he was dancing all over the road while he banged haphazardly at the drum and swigged back whiskey from a bottle. It was great entertainment.

Next came a band made up of drummers and pipers. They were mostly young men wearing tartan kilts and hats. Every now and then the drummers stopped drumming for a few seconds and put their drumsticks up their noses. It seemed an odd thing to do, but they all did it in unison, so I guessed it must have been part of their performance.

The sound of the band was glorious. It made my heart swell with pride, although I had nothing to be proud of. The loud beat of the drums was like a drug, making my feet want to start marching. I now realised why drummer boys were used to lead men to war. I wanted to march with them, but I thought I'd wait to see Brenda in her orange dress first.

More banners swayed in the air as the men shouted proclamations of loyalty to King Billy and derogatory comments about the Pope. They were working themselves up into a fine state before marching through the predominantly Catholic area of Marsh Lane where another Battle of the Boyne was about to take place. King Billy and his queen were behind the banners. He looked a bit like a pantomime performer in his stockings and long curly wig. He was obviously quite drunk and staggered along the road waving his sceptre at the spectators as though he really was some inebriated old king.

Then I saw Brenda walking with the women. The older women wore two-piece suits with an orange sash and the girls wore long, orange dresses. Some of the girls looked tired, marching out of step, holding their dresses up to their knees as though they were wading through water. I called out to Brenda and she came over to me. She said there was going to be trouble at Marsh Lane and I should stay at the back with the women. On hearing that I raced forward, anxious not to miss anything. As I was probably in for a hiding that night from my dad, I decided to make the most of it.

A Dandelion By Any Other Name

I wasn't going to miss anything, especially the fight.

I ran to the front where the men in bowler hats were just approaching the huge jeering crowd that had gathered on the corner of Marsh Lane. People in the crowd were swearing and yelling insults at the marchers as they strutted past. Policemen on horseback lined that bit of road. They knew from experience that if there was going to be trouble, this is where it would happen. I'd never noticed before how big horses' arses were. They reminded me of Mrs MacBride. She was a teacher at school.

The drums gave a great roll, then all the Orangemen broke into a song about the 'fucking Pope'. Their marching turned into an unsynchronised jigging. Obscenities, mainly consisting of the words 'fuckin' bastards' exploded in the air. Eggs, bits of rotten fruit and stones were flying about, hitting people from all directions. Women at the front of the crowd deliberately raised small crucifixes from around their necks and pointed them at the parade as though they were protecting themselves from vampires. One man chucked some bright-green confetti into the procession. The Orangemen reacted as if it were dung that had been thrown. The colour of the confetti upset them more than the rotten fruit, and they retaliated by raising their fists at the crowd, calling them Catholic cowards. The big man with the big drum was spoiling for a fight as he began yelling something about Mary (the Lord's mother) being a whore.

On the pavement, the horses were pushed aside as some of the angry onlookers rushed into the road to defend the dignity of their religion from the Orange blasphemers. The inevitable fight erupted. Men were rolling about in the road, punching each other in bodies and heads. The policemen tried to break up the fighting, but the drummers and the pipers were running to help their fellow Orangemen at the front. The scene where Stanley Road crossed Marsh Lane corner was chaotic. Banners were ripped and drums rolled along the road. For a moment I thought of Mr Rainer's head rolling in the gutter with his eyebrows still going up and down, the head looking at me telling me to carry on with the game lovey, while his body marched on somewhere further down Stanley Road. The poor horses were in the middle of the road, twirling about like the Spanish Riding School out of control. The police were pelted with missiles along with the marchers. I saw one man, who was close enough for me to hear the thud of bone against bone, head-butt another man in the face causing his nose to pour with blood. As the bloody man fell forward he was repeatedly kicked in the head by two others.

I turned away in sickened disgust. Suddenly a heavy hand came down on my shoulder. Looking up I saw the angry, familiar old face of my dad. Still wearing his work clothes, he escorted me roughly away from the crowd, down the bottom end of Marsh Lane and along Bank Road towards Berry Street. All the time he never loosened his grip on me and he never spoke. It was as though he were saving all his vehemence for later. I was under parental arrest and would be punished accordingly.

The repulsive, violent sight I'd witnessed remained with me as my dad pushed me through the front door of our house. Only then did he let go of my arm. A strapping with a leather belt across the legs seemed so much more civilised than the wild, uncontrolled violence I'd just encountered. Although a strapping with my dad's belt stung for hours, it was preferable to being bashed in the face by a fist, a head or a boot. I stood meekly in our living room, cowering, waiting for the imminent thrashing. But he simply sat down at the table while my mum placed his tea before him.

For some reason my dad never gave me the belting I had

A Dandelion By Any Other Name

expected. He told me I was never to go out without his permission again, and I was to keep away from Brenda Rainer and the Orange Lodge. I wondered how he knew I was friends with Brenda. The gossips in the corner shop must have told him. One or two women liked to talk to my dad when they spotted him getting off his bike outside our house. One woman always asked him for a ciggy and he would always find one to give her.

My mum told me later that people were saying Brenda earned her pocket money down at the bus station – wanking the busmen for three shillings a go during the week and charging double for weekends. I didn't believe it. The gossips were out to discredit Brenda any way they could. Nevertheless, I didn't go back over to Brenda's house for a long time. It was her dog Billy I missed the most. And the free ice-creams.

6

A Dead Unmoving Thing

During the school holidays my dad decided to take us somewhere special. We thought it might be to Blackpool, Rhyl or Southport, or maybe a ferry ride across to New Brighton. But it was none of these. We were to visit a place called Ramsbottom. We were setting off on a holy pilgrimage to the town, which, apart from the spelling, was our namesake. I could tell my mum didn't want to go. She hardly ever wanted to go on any of my dad's planned outings. But she got herself ready anyway, wearing a black raincoat and scarf as though she were off to a funeral.

My dad smoothed Brylcreem on his hair and put on his best tweed cap. He must have been planning the trip for some time, meticulously doing his homework on the train and bus timetables, as the journey to Ramsbottom entailed one bus ride and three different train rides.

At a quarter past nine on a Saturday morning, the five members of the Rammsbottom family left Berry Street, destination: Ramsbottom. Cushla had insisted on bringing a bucket and spade, even though there was no beach there. We boarded the familiar green Southport-to-Liverpool train at Bootle station.

Through the train window we could see all the old docks along the Liverpool waterfront. The first part of our journey (from Bootle to Liverpool) made three stops at run-down deserted stations and then onto the terminus in town.

Only half an hour after leaving home my mum's 'gasping for a cup of tea' began. In his elaborate schedule my dad had not planned tea breaks and hurried us along to catch the next train at Lime Street station. Cushla complained that her legs were hurting. My dad called her a whining little bitch as he lifted her up, her bucket and spade dangling down over his shoulder. Then Janet wanted to go to the toilet.

'Can't yer bloody well wait?' my dad said. He was cursing us under his breath, saying it was like taking a tribe of Arabs out. In retaliation Janet swung into foot-dragging mode. Being described as a tribe of Arabs caused my mum to start sniggering. Normally I enjoyed it when she became one of us against my dad, but not this day.

Apart from my dad, I seemed to be the only one with any enthusiasm for going to Ramsbottom. I was interested in finding out what sort of people would choose to live in a place with that name. Maybe our name was common there and not the laughing stock it was in Liverpool. Maybe we could live there.

But we never arrived. We missed the next train by seconds. My dad complained to the ticket collector, disgusted that he hadn't held the train up while Janet was having a pee in the toilet. 'How dare you treat a British working man like that!' he yelled at the Indian guard who had blown the whistle for the train to depart. By one o'clock we were all back home in Berry Street. My mum was pleased to be back as she had planned to go to the bingo that evening and was worrying that she might not be home in time. She enjoyed going to the bingo, and often came home with prizes such as a box of glasses, or a set of pillow cases with little embroidered flowers on them.

As well as evenings out to the bingo, my mum liked to visit spiritualists. Her spiritual life was a strange, contradictory thing. She spurned orthodox religion but wanted to believe in something, so spiritualism seemed to fill the gap. And visiting spiritualists was a popular pastime for many people, especially women. Mrs Potter performed sessions on a Saturday night in Waterloo. She lived in a big weather-beaten house with large bay windows overlooking the River Mersey. The service was performed in the front parlour with the curtains drawn and only a dim red lamp for lighting. People would sit in a circle while Mrs Potter passed on messages from beyond the grave. My mum didn't seem to think much of her, but continued to go for a while before she heard of a better one called Mrs Gladstone who lived in Litherland.

My dad hardly ever went out in the evenings, but he didn't object to my mum's social whirl at the bingo halls, spiritualists and jumble sales. When she came home from her circle at the spiritualist's, my dad would ask her if she'd had any luck. Most of the time she would crinkle her nose and shake her head. I could never understand what it was she hoped to hear. 'It's just bullshit,' my dad would say and my mum would agree.

One Saturday night in August, I accompanied my mum to Mrs Potter's house in Waterloo. It was teeming rain and there was a rumble of thunder in the distance. We caught the 6.30 train, and fifteen minutes later we were outside the large, three-storey house. The rain fell steadily and a mist hung over the river like a grey veil. Although it was perfect weather for a seance, many of the regulars hadn't turned up. There were only two other women, an old man,

Mrs Potter and us. Six of us – the Devil's number. We each payed two shillings to be part of this adventure.

Mrs Potter was a woman of about fifty. I noticed she had a lot of make-up and rouge on her face, which made her look like one of those Punch and Judy puppets. Her bright red lips and thin pencil eyebrows reminded me of Bette Davis, the older version. Beneath the make-up Mrs Potter's face looked as weather-beaten as her house. Her fat fingers displayed a variety of large ruby rings. I had never seen anybody wearing a ring on their little finger before. I wondered if that's what rich people do. She certainly looked rich.

We all sat in a circle around a table covered in a white tablecloth with a red lamp above us. The softer glow made the spiritualist appear less doll-like. One of the women put her glasses on to make sure she missed nothing, even though we were asked to close our eyes. I felt a wave of tingling excitement down my spine, similar to when a horror film is about to start, except this was real. Here we were sitting in a front parlour in Waterloo, about to make contact with souls from the other side, people who could tell us what it was like being dead and were capable of warning us of our earthly futures.

After a short prayer, we all held hands. It was nice being able to hold my mum's cool hand, but the hand on the other side of me belonged to the old man. He smelt of sweaty socks and kept pulling his hand away to rub the end of his nose with his thumb and forefinger. Then he would take hold of my hand again.

In the dim light, I noticed it was only Mrs Potter who continued to close her eyes. The rest of us were on full alert, waiting for the messages. There was a short silence, then Mrs Potter began chanting 'Edward' in a deep voice. One of the other women repeated the name and looked about the table for somebody to claim Edward.

'I know an Edgar,' said the old man.

'It's close enough,' said the woman with the glasses. 'Was he ever called Edward, or Eddy?'

'I suppose he could have been,' said the man, wiping another dewdrop from the end of his nose.

'That's it then,' said the woman. 'This'll be for you.'

Mrs Potter relayed the message from Edward or Edgar to the old man. The message was that he should eat plenty of greens.

There were other messages. A spirit called Anne warned the woman wearing the glasses to watch out for her handbag. Another message from a John said that somebody beginning with S would win some money on the bingo. It wouldn't be much but it would come in handy. There were other similar messages. Does the number seven mean anything to anybody? A birthday? A house number? The letter G? The month of July perhaps? Anything?

There was nothing for my mum. Mrs Potter came out of her trance and said a closing prayer.

On the way back to Waterloo station we stopped at a fish-and-chip shop. While we waited for our shilling's worth of chips and two fish, I pondered the ethereal messages that had transcended the barriers of time and space. Why didn't they tell us what it's like being dead? Is there a God? Do people really go to heaven and hell? Will there be another world war? My mum decided never to go back to Mrs Potter's house. She said the woman was a charlatan and only made things up for the money. Mrs Gladstone from Litherland would be better.

The fish and chips were salty, hot and delicious. We sat on a wooden bench in the station and ate them from the newspaper wrapping. As I licked the salt from my fingers, I remembered with a shiver of disgust the old man and his runny nose. The green train came rattling through the blackness of the tunnel into the station. By the time we were back in Berry Street the rain had stopped and there were light patches breaking in the dull sky.

That night I made Janet and Cushla hold hands in the darkness of the parlour while I pronounced the name Rammsbottom in a deep sighing voice. They didn't think much of the new game and complained bitterly when they detected the smell of fish and chips on my breath.

With such a comic surname it was inevitable that I should develop into the role of classroom clown. Yet strangely enough, I was always near the top of the A stream, and two years in a row I came top of the class.

I now had a couple of friends, Valerie and Joan. They called me Bottom for short, and it was easier to just go along with it than to insist on something better. When we read *A Midsummer Night's Dream* I came across the only other character I knew of in the world called Bottom, and he was an ass.

After a particularly bad day at school I would come home and berate my mum for marrying a man with such a name. For not considering how it might affect the children. She just laughed and told me not to be so bloody soft. 'There's nothink wrong with the name,' she'd say.

'Try tellin' that to everybody at school,' I protested. 'Ask them what's wrong with them. Why do they laugh if there's nothink wrong?' She never answered me when I said that. She knew what she had done and tried to pretend it didn't matter.

Secondary school was for girls who had failed the eleven-plus exam. I had deliberately performed poorly during the test, making sure I wouldn't have to go to the grammar school. Girls who went to the grammar school had to wear old-fashioned hats and were called toffs. Many a day I spent lounging about at home when I should have been at school. I would lie on the couch and look up at the cracks in the ceiling. I could spend a whole day just lying about like that, thinking and imagining a completely different world. I was lucky: my mum didn't mind me staying away from school now and again to loll about. She could probably see that in some way I'd taken after her, and escape from reality was a necessity rather than an indulgence.

At the beginning of April (a few weeks before my twelfth birthday) a young policeman with gangly long legs came to our door to tell my mum that her husband was dead. It was no surprise. My dad had been admitted to Bootle Hospital for an operation. The doctors had cut him open and then stitched him up again without removing anything. His skin had turned yellow and my mum said she could smell the cancer when she visited him after the operation.

My last memory of my dad was saying goodbye to him in the hospital. It was the evening before his operation and he was crying like a baby, holding onto my mum. I'd never seen a man cry before. It made me want to cry too. My mum just sat there like a statue on his bed looking at the wall while he clung to her. It was hard to interpret the expression on her face. It could have been pity or disgust. It was probably indifference.

The day he died, a new three-piece suite arrived. It was black shiny vinyl with orange moquette cushions with a four-seater couch and two chairs. My mum had bought the suite in anticipation of the insurance payout and to accommodate people for sandwiches and tea after the funeral. It was a Tuesday, and outside the rain fell heavily and consistently.

The new modern lounge suite was exciting, as was all the

attention we were suddenly getting. Bereavement brought a certain prestige. Many of the houses in the street had their curtains drawn throughout the day as a sign of respect. Mrs O'Flynn from across the road had bought a box of cakes from Blackledges for us, and a man from my dad's work had given my mum the proceeds of the dockers' whip-round: £71/4/6d. The dockers were never mean with their money.

As we sat on the new settee, three young fatherless girls eating jam doughnuts, the coffin arrived. My dad had come home for the last time. Some men set him up in the front parlour as we crowded round like spectators trying to catch a glimpse of a celebrity. Cushla was jumping up and down with excitement, cake crumbs flying everywhere. The front parlour table was extended to accommodate the large rosewood coffin.

Still munching on our doughnuts we went in to see the body. The lid was off and he was dressed in a long white nightie surrounded by the white silk lining of the coffin. My mum removed the cloth covering his face. Janet and I started to giggle. Not because we were pleased to see our father dead, but because the situation seemed so absurd: that he, the person we knew as dad, should be dressed like that lying in a box on the table in our front parlour. Like a Christmas decoration.

The curtains were drawn, leaving the room in semi-darkness. My mum stood looking at him, her lips compressed tightly. She slowly moved her head from side to side taking him in from different angles. Cushla started banging the brass handles of the coffin against the wood as though she were ratta-tat-tatting on a door.

'Stop that!' my mum snapped at her.

'Why? Will it wake him up?' asked Cushla.

'He's dead, yer never wake up once yer dead,' I explained.

'Lazarus did,' said Janet.

'That's all made up, that is. Isn't it mum?' I said, looking at my widowed mother for confirmation. But she said nothing. She lifted Cushla up to see the body. After Cushla was satisfied that it was her dad in the box and he had now become a dead unmoving thing, they both left the room.

When the nervous giggly stage subsided, Janet and I had a good look at the body. I pulled one of the curtains back to let in some daylight over the coffin. We'd seen dead bodies before when people in the street had died. My dad's face looked the same as it usually did except he was perfectly motionless, not moving or breathing. His hands looked much the same, the fingernails still dirty and the middle and forefinger were yellow with nicotine. But he was also different. Death had daubed him with some waxy new impression. I touched his nose, which was cold and slightly rigid, and there was cotton wool up both nostrils. His forehead was hard and cold like marble.

I knew that dead human flesh rots the same way dead animals do, and after a few days it begins to stink and decay. Sometimes I'd stand and gaze at meat in the butcher's shop window and think that could be me there on that plate. If I got minced up, I'd look like that. My poor dad. Where had the man I knew as my dad gone to? It was his exterior, but there was no one in it. What a strange thing to happen to people. One minute you're a warm-bodied living person wondering how or why you managed to be here in the first place, and then you're a lump of rotting meat. Gone forever. No wonder we need some comfort – Jesus on the cross or the ramblings of a spiritualist.

Janet tried to open one of the body's eyes. Most of the white, which had now turned yellow, was showing and a bit of the pupil. But when she tried to push the eyelid down, it would only go half-way and part of the eyeball was left exposed. It was not from ghoulishness that we continued to explore the immensity of death in our front parlour, but sheer curiosity. Almost a scientific curiosity. There was a little golliwog brooch (free in exchange for marmalade labels) on the parlour mantelpiece and I decided to find out if a corpse would bleed if it was pierced with a pin. It didn't. Cushla came back into the room. She pulled a chair next to the coffin and stood up on it. Bending over the remains of her father, she continued to eat yet another cake. A lamington. 'He's dead now, isn't he?' she said, completely nonchalant.

She saw me touching his face, my fingers more inquisitive than loving. Janet was still attempting to close the eyelid. 'I wanna touch,' said Cushla putting the cake in her other hand and pulling the corpse's nose with her right hand.

'Not like that!' I said pushing her back roughly. She started to cry.

Suddenly the corpse's hand was raised in the air by Janet, who was imitating his voice, calling us bloody peevish bitches. Cushla went off crying to my mum, who came in to see what we were up to. 'What the hellavyer done?' she said, seeing her dead husband's nose pushed to one side, cotton wool falling half way out of his left nostril and one eye prised open. 'Jesus, have some bloody respect!' My mum put the cloth back over his face, closed the curtain and chased us out of the room. We had to wash our hands in case we caught the cancer.

That night our Aunty Ella came to stay with us. She was to sleep in the double bed with my mum as there was nowhere else for her to go other than on the new settee, but that would mean sleeping downstairs amongst the dead. I loved her staying with us. She was my dad's sister and she never stopped talking. Aunty Ella was a self-appointed authority on almost every subject under the sun and she had the perfect listener in our taciturn mother.

We all sat up late into the night, except Cushla, who was curled up asleep on one of the new chairs. Janet and I were allowed to have a small sherry with the women. They were talking about operations, funerals, death rattles and different types of cancer. Then Aunty Ella started telling my mum about death calls. She said that when the poison gas comes out of their bodies, corpses sometimes sit up in the night and call out. They make a deep aaarrhhh sound – 'they can't help it you see, Lily' – and don't mean to frighten anybody.

By eleven o'clock the sherry bottle was empty and we were all laughing at what Aunty Ella was saying about the Queen. She told us there was an automatic bum-wiper in the royal toilet at Buckingham Palace. She said the Queen only had to press a button and a mechanical hand bearing toilet paper (the colour and pattern of the Union Jack) came out of the wall to perform the royal task. For many years to come I wondered if Aunty Ella was having us on or not. I felt sorry for the Queen every time I saw her on TV. Such an appliance seemed more an inconvenience than a luxury to me.

When the time came for us to go to bed, I gently closed the parlour door before going upstairs. I didn't want to hear any death calls in the night. Having a real corpse lying downstairs in the house at night suddenly became frightening. Things change in the dark. You can't trust the metamorphosis of the secret night. It has its own powers.

In bed I could hear Aunty Ella still talking to my mum in the next bedroom and making her laugh. They were both laughing out loud. Although neither Janet nor I could hear what they were laughing at, the mirth was contagious and we giggled along with them.

I liked hearing my mum laugh. There's an old saying – if you laugh today, you'll cry tomorrow. Would she be crying tomorrow? The day of the funeral? I thought of my poor dad, disappeared off the face of the earth with just his shell left lying on its own downstairs in a house full of cackling females. From the bedroom window I could see a solitary star shining in the cold sky, like a silver button on a navy blue coat. For a moment, I imagined my dad had somehow gone to live up there on that star, as a spirit existing in a different dimension to us. I whispered 'I'm sorry' to the star, and then got up to draw the curtains. I wanted to cry but I bit my lip hard. There was the unspoken female law in our house, a law that discouraged any display of affection, physically or emotionally. Just as my mum seemed indifferent to us, we extended that apparent nonchalance to each other. No hugging, no kisses, no apologies and definitely no tears for each other. My mum shed tears for young Roddy McCorley but never for us.

In the morning a variety of neighbours, relatives and my dad's workmates came to pay their last respects. They all looked at the body and said he was at peace now. Perfect peace. Wreaths of flowers were arriving and were placed next to the coffin in the parlour. Our Aunty Irene bought us black veils to wear as we didn't have much in the way of black clothes.

I loved my veil. I practised a mournful expression in the mirror, my sad eyes accentuated by the dark wispy veil. It may not have been as pretty as the Catholic girls' white communion veils I'd coveted a few years back, but it was an acceptable, more sophisticated substitute. The black mourning veil had an element of mystery to it which eclipsed the white confirmation veils. It was like wearing black nylon stockings instead of white ankle socks.

In Berry Street a funeral, like a wedding, was a source of public interest. It was two o'clock in the afternoon and already there was a gathering of spectators outside our house, waiting to see the coffin carried into the hearse and to examine the faces of the mourners. The number and quality of wreaths would be commented upon later, as would the contents of the sandwiches.

The sky was overcast with the threat of rain as six men in suits struggled to carry the closed coffin from the parlour into the narrow lobby and out through the front door. The pallbearers were made up of my dad's fellow dockers. Behind the hearse were two shiny black cars for the mourners. The voices in the street hushed as the coffin was carried into the waiting hearse. A familiar voice called out 'Rest in peace, Harry'. It belonged to Maggie Fox from Canal Street, the woman who had always managed to cadge a spare Woodbine from my dad. She would miss him.

The moment arrived when the bereaved family had to walk out before a gaze of onlookers. Janet and I started to giggle nervously as we checked our veils. Mrs Gawler and Mrs O'Flynn would be out there studying our expressions, and it would be terrible to be caught giggling. My mum had a little black hat on and she held Cushla's hand as they stepped out into the street. My mum looked no sadder than usual. There were no tears. Janet and I followed behind, our faces half-covered with handkerchiefs and our shoulders shaking uncontrollably. People thought we were crying and called out for God to bless us. Aunty Ella and Aunty Irene escorted us into the car. 'He's at peace now, Lily,' Aunty Ella said, more to console herself than my mum.

The wreaths were laid out across the coffin, and the car behind us was occupied by the men in suits. All three vehicles started moving slowly forward along Berry Street towards Thornton cemetery. People we recognised and those we'd never seen before stopped in their tracks as we drove past. Many people made the sign of the cross and men removed their caps as they stood watching.

It was as though we had suddenly transformed into a royal procession. I was a princess, the eldest daughter, heir to the throne. I wanted to perform a royal wave as I passed all my revering subjects, but thought better of it as Aunty Ella was sitting opposite me. In the driver's mirror I sneaked a glance at my immaculately placed veil. I looked magnificent. Just then the driver began to speak. He was addressing my mum by her surname, an unwelcome sound that caused the Royal House of Rammsbottom to evaporate.

At two-thirty, as my dad's coffin was lowered into the ground at Thornton cemetery, it started to rain again. There's a saying about rain at a funeral: it's a sign that the departed one is happy and at peace. This divine evidence precipitated a fresh recital of comments regarding the peace, the perfect peace. Umbrellas opened and the balding vicar slowly read out a few words while we all stared at the oblong hole in the earth where my dad, lying inside a wooden box, had been lowered. The name Harold William Rammsbottom was uttered, and stood out amid the stream of religious blather like a 'Fuck off!' yelled in a library. The solemnity of the occasion was replaced by embarrassment and inward sniggering. I bet even Saint Peter would be hard put not to have a quiet titter when reading the name out (with three M's) as my dad floated towards the pearly gates. After the collective amen, we each had a last look at the ground before walking quietly back to the cars and home for the ham sandwiches and tea.

From that day on, life would never be the same. With my mum's easy-going ways or indifference (whatever it could be called), there was a new freedom for us to do exactly as we liked. Being the eldest, I decided I would take over as man of the house.

A Dandelion By Any Other Name

Somehow in the not-too-distant future I'd rid myself of the terrible name and my real, my true life would begin. My plan was simple enough. I decided my mum would have to quickly remarry; that way we could cash in on our new dad's name. There was a widower over the road called Stan Mitchell. He was a scruffy, doddery old fellow, but what did that matter? My mum could stay in the kitchen enjoying herself, singing away on her own. What did matter, though, was he had a normal-sounding name, and if my mum played her cards right, I could soon be Deirdre Mitchell. An ordinary, normal type of person.

7

The Blackman

The day after my dad's funeral, the neighbourhood curtains opened again, signalling a return to normality. Very quickly we adjusted to being an all-female family. My mum received a widow's pension, which wasn't much to keep four of us on, but she seemed to manage quite well. The Sunday chocolate cake was now cut into four peaceful quarters. The black-and-orange lounge suite was accompanied by a new wooden coffee table (although we only ever drank tea), and soft pink rolls of toilet tissue were placed on top of the cistern in the lavatory. The harsh, inefficient newspaper squares were thrown out, never to be used again. A new era was emerging: a period of modernisation and freedom.

The kitchen sink was still the only means of having a wash. Water was boiled in a kettle and poured into the plastic orange bowl in the sink. This bowl was used for washing our bodies, washing clothes, peeling potatoes and drowning kittens.

The cat we had before Tiger was a female. Her name was Kitty, and Tiger was one of her sons. When she gave birth to six kittens we were allowed to watch them grow for a few weeks, and delighted in their playfulness. But one Sunday evening at about seven o'clock the orange bowl was filled with cold water. My dad had kept five struggling little bundles under the water with his knife. I thought he was stabbing them but he was drowning them. Janet and I crowded round to watch. I cried for them not to be hurt, expecting to see the clear water turn red with blood. 'Get these bloody bitches out of the way' he had yelled to my mum as another little head bobbed to the surface to breath and make a tiny miaowing sound.

A few weeks later Kitty disappeared and our only remaining pet was little Tiger. My mum had taken Kitty to the RSPCA to be put down for committing the inevitable crime of becoming pregnant.

My mum continued to be emotionally detached, and hardly ever placed constraints on us. It seemed we were free to do whatever we liked. The old doddery widower, Stan Mitchell from across the road, wasn't a bit interested in marrying my mum, nor she in marrying him. They hardly ever acknowledged each other's existence. I tried to make conversation with him, volunteering to do his shopping, but he only told me to 'fuck off out of it!'

Mitchell. It was a shame to see such a good name wasted.

Tommy Patterson (my young uncle) would sometimes come over to our house after school. He lived with Nanny (my mum's mother), who gave him whatever he wanted. As far as I knew, his wants only stretched to lemonade, chocolate and comics. He was football crazy and made me try to dribble a ball with him in our backyard, perform headers and tackle him. But I wasn't a bit interested in learning the finer skills of football and was pleased when he would eventually have to go. There was a rule decreeing he had to be gone before my dad arrived home.

But with my dad now gone Tommy started coming over every Friday to help us eat our fish and chips. He didn't have to disappear at five o'clock anymore, so he sometimes stayed until eight o'clock. He was fifteen, and like most older lads was fanatical about football. He supported Everton rather than Liverpool and always wore a blue-and-white scarf wherever he went. Soon he started visiting us more than once a week. He came on Wednesdays and Saturdays too. He always came on his own as his mother (our Nanny) hardly ever left her house. She was Irish, but she never pined after her homeland the way many did. Like Tommy, her wants were few. She liked a bottle of Guinness every day with her tea, and two daily newspapers to read: the *Daily Mirror* in the morning and the *Liverpool Echo* in the evening. Like most Irish mothers, she adored her sons, especially Tommy. Whenever he left the house, whether to go to school or to play football, she prayed to God for his safety. He seemed to be the sole reason for her existence.

I resented Tommy visiting us so often. Now that my dad wasn't there to frighten him off, he took advantage. If anybody was to take over as 'man of the house' it was going to be me.

The day other people call Guy Fawkes was known in Bootle as Bonfire Night. For about a week before the fifth of November, children and adults collected anything that was unwanted and burnable for the 'bommy'. A pyramid of rubbish at the back of the prefabs increased by the day. Every year on the fifth the bommy was set ablaze and every year the fire brigade was called out by frightened residents. Guys were made from old clothes. Some just looked like lumpy scarecrows; others were more elaborately created, wearing real shoes and socks with a hangman's rope around their necks. There was a similarity in their expressions – that of the passive fool staring vaguely ahead with an idiotic smile. Once a year the guys enjoyed their few days of simple glory, oblivious to the terrible fiery fate that awaited them.

There was something cruel and medieval about that time of year. It reminded me of pictures I'd seen in history books at school: bodies in gibbets and people burned to death at the stake. Most guys sat propped up in old prams or were strapped to trolleys while children wheeled them to street corners, pestering each passer-by for a penny.

On the afternoon before the bonfire, Tommy brought a bag of fireworks round to our house. They consisted mainly of bangers and riff-raffs. I hated them. Lads seemed to love them. Just walking to and from school became more traumatic than usual. In the streets lads enjoyed throwing fireworks at screaming girls. The more we screamed and jumped the more they revelled in it. I hated the noisy bangs and the unpredictable riff-raffs that whizzed and leaped about trying to jump up skirts.

Tommy was in our back yard lighting his fireworks one at a time, and then four or five simultaneously for a louder, bigger explosion. Janet and Cushla were upstairs watching him from the safety of the bedroom window. I was downstairs complaining about the noisy male intrusion into our female domain. I could tell my mum hated the bangs as much as I did, but she said to let him be, he was just a lad enjoying himself. But it wasn't fair. Lads seemed to have societal permission to torment others, in the street, in school and now at home, simply because they were inconsiderate louts.

In retaliation for this injustice, I filled the mop bucket with water and stepped into the back yard where Tommy was blasting the air with dynamite. I grabbed his brown paper bag of fireworks from off the window-sill and dunked it into the bucket of water. I kept it under the water making sure the contents were completely soaked, the way my dad made sure the kittens were completely drowned. When Tommy realised what I'd done he howled with rage and tried to thump me, but I ran back into the kitchen, bolting the door behind me. He banged his fists on the window until my mum opened the door and let him in. When he showed her his dripping wet bag of treasures, explaining in gasps how I'd deliberately ruined them, she turned on me like a mother cat. I said I didn't want him coming to our house anymore, that I hated the fireworks and the football.

My mum's face became a deep red colour as her anger surfaced. She screamed at me, calling me a selfish bitch before tears made her words unintelligible. Tommy went off home in a huff while my mum sat down in an armchair and cried strange animal sounds into her hanky. She told me to take three shillings from her purse and run after Tommy, so he could buy some more fireworks.

It was dangerous for a girl to be out on her own on the fifth of November, and I was reluctant to follow him. But when I saw how upset my mum was I decided to run the gauntlet of banger-throwing lads. I ran almost all the way to Nanny's house without catching sight of Tommy and without being attacked. Tommy wasn't there, only Nanny, who immediately started worrying and fingering her rosary beads. 'God bless my little Tommy.'

I told her what had happened, how I'd upset Tommy, and gave her the three shillings for him to buy more. I told her my mum had been crying because of what I'd done to Tommy's fireworks. 'It's taken a bloody long time for her to do that,' said Nanny mumbling curses under her breath. 'Yer know she give him away, don't yer? Said she didn't want him, a four-year-old baby! Didn't want him because of that blackman.'

Nanny was always saying things like that, providing mysterious little bits of information that never made much sense. I'd worked out from previous ramblings that The Blackman must be my dad, but he had never been black, none of us were black. I asked her what she meant, hoping she might explain something I could comprehend. If I had Negro blood in my veins, I wanted to know about it. Then she told me, very matter of factly without the rambling innuendo, that Tommy was my mum's firstborn. His father was an American soldier who never knew about the pregnancy. Up to the age of four years old Tommy lived with the two women. While my mum worked in a sausage factory, Nanny looked after the child. 'He was a lovely baby, not a bit of trouble.'

Then one night, my mum met my dad. That was when she became pregnant a second time – with me. He said he didn't want Tommy living with them when they married. Nanny unofficially adopted him and raised him as her own. 'A four-year-old baby and she give him away.'

So I had a brother. Tommy was a brother, not an uncle. A mixture of pride, guilt and fear washed over me. 'Why hasn't nobody ever told us?' I asked.

'Cos of that fuckin' mean-hearted bugger she went and married.'

'D'yer mean me dad?' I asked, not liking her saying such things.

'Yis, I do. It was because of carryin' you that she done it.'

'How can it be my fault?' I could feel tears coming. It was as though a dead body had been found in a shallow grave and the prime suspect for the murder appeared to be me.

'It's not your fault, it's hers,' my grandmother explained, pointing her finger in the direction of Berry Street. 'She can't keep her leg off the bloody dustbin.'

'What dustbin?' I asked becoming confused again.

'In the back-entry, where d'yer think?'

I guessed now what she might be meaning, but my voice was

too quivery with emotion to ask for a clearer translation. Nanny started poking at the coals in the fire. She was a thin woman with a sallow complexion and dark eyes. Kids in the street used to call her a witch. I suppose it must have hurt her, because she went outside less and less until eventually she didn't leave the house at all. Tommy now did all the shopping.

'While he was alive, no one could say nothink,' she said, putting the wire-mesh fireguard back. 'But now he's dead, it's got to come out.'

I stared at the three empty cups on the table. They were chipped and one of them had no handle. Tea stains had changed the interiors from white to streaky brown. The all-important slice of raw onion was placed at the centre of the table, warding off germs and evil spirits. Nobody could say we weren't a good germ-fearing family. The onion may have kept away germs, but it certainly didn't work with fleas. Little black fleas jumped about the dusty floor in excitement. They didn't get many visitors, so my presence announced a potential meal of fresh young blood.

Nanny sat on a heap of old newspapers that had accumulated on an armchair. It must have felt uncomfortable but it didn't seem to bother her. She wasn't the typical grandmother portrayed on TV programmes or in films – the ones with grey hair tied up in a bun, wearing a clean apron, cheerily making apple pies. This one was a mixture of the sacred and profane. She drank Guinness and wasn't timid about using the fuck word, even in prayers. God was understanding. And she never baked anything, ever. It was always a packet of digestive biscuits and a cup of strong tea whenever we visited. But today, I was offered neither. 'Yer better get off home now, it's gettin' dark out there,' she said, getting up to see me out. 'My poor Tommy, I hope to God he's safe.'

Her voice changed from being angry to a snivelling pleading to

God. 'God bless my little Tommy,' she whined at the ceiling while fingering her rosary beads. If God does listen to prayers, He must have been sick of hearing her repetitious pleas.

'Does Tommy know that me mum's his real mother?' I asked.

'Yis, he knows, God love him. He's always known his mam give him up, never wanted him, swapped him for a blackman.' I closed the door behind me without saying the usual 'taraa'. It was about four o'clock and already the air had the chill of a winter evening. I could smell smoke from early bonfires and the nitre of fireworks, which were starting to explode everywhere. They produced sharp cracks and fizzing sounds in the nearby streets and distant little booms from all over town, like a miniature war.

As I walked back there was an ache in my heart. It was for my mum, for my dad, for Tommy and myself, then it extended to everything before me. For life itself. I thought about how Bootle was hit hard by the German air raids in the real war and hundreds of people were killed huddling for safety in the air-raid shelters. As I turned into Marsh Lane, I met Tommy. He saw me but didn't say anything. 'Me mum sent three bob for more fireworks,' I said. 'I give it to Nanny for yer.'

'There's no more left in the shops at this hour,' he said, his lip curling slightly in anger. I'd never really looked at him before. He had black wavy hair and dark-blue eyes. He looked more Irish than any of us. He was actually quite handsome. My brother. I wanted to touch him, but that was out of the question. Any expression of affection was a sign of weakness.

'I'm sorry for what I done,' I whispered, my eyes starting to fill again with tears. Nobody in our family had ever apologised to the other. It was an unwritten law.

'It doesn't matter,' he said, looking at the ground as he shuffled his feet. He seemed to be feeling awkward, probably because of my staring at him with such intensity. 'They were only fireworks,' he said magnanimously. I could feel a tear rolling down my cheek. 'Come on, I'll walk yer back to Berry Street.'

'No, Nanny's worryin' about yer. I can run back on me own.' I turned away, more from embarrassment than an eagerness to get home, and I ran. I ran without stopping until I was in Berry Street. A gang of lads on the corner had thrown a couple of bangers at me, but I didn't provide them with the fun they were after. I just kept running without screaming or looking back.

At home, Janet and Cushla were dissecting the cardboard remains of Tommy's fireworks in the back yard. Their hands were black from the sludgy powder. My mum was peeling potatoes in the kitchen. She had stopped crying but she wasn't singing either. I wondered if she'd tried to rid herself of Tommy before he was born, as she had with me. I bet she had.

Tommy and I now had something in common. As well as both being born on Wednesdays, which made us children of woe, we were probably both conceived on the same dustbin too. And we had managed to survive the gin and mustard bath. If I was Deirdre, the stubborn little bitch, brother Tommy was even worse. He was a stubborn little bastard. But he had a normal name – Tommy Patterson – and I didn't. My mum had been Lily Patterson before she married that man, the blackman with the awful name who inflicted sorrow and shame in all directions. My poor, cruel, kind-hearted dad who was never shown a scrap of affection by any of us, except maybe Cushla, when she sat on his knee on Sunday evenings. She was his favourite.

After tea, Janet and I walked over to see the Berry Street bonfire. This was the first time we'd ever been allowed to go on our own. In the past my dad had either escorted us or forbidden us to go. The fire was already blazing when we arrived. About a hundred people were standing round it, their faces lit up like stage performers by the yellow flames. The heat of the fire felt luxurious at first, then my face became too hot for comfort. The flames were mesmerising to watch. There's something primitive about people standing round a fire. It seems to evoke a distant memory, something still there in the genes recalling pagan roots.

Fireworks were going off all about. Young girls linked arms with their mothers, making them physical extensions of the adults. This limited the lads to throwing their bangers into the fire.

People cheered noisily as the guys were thrown, each in their turn, onto the crackling blaze. It was grisly to watch. The vacant smiling face of a guy was visible for a few seconds amongst the flames before bending forward in a farewell bow to the audience. Turning black, he quickly disintegrated and became part of the fire. I thought about the witches burnt at the stake in the Middle Ages. Women were dragged from their homes accused of being in league with the Devil. I imagined the horrible deaths they must have suffered. And the women of Salem in the seventeenth century, condemned by children as witches and burnt alive. No anaesthetics – death was the only release from the agony. Mothers, sisters, daughters, grandmothers. The families later poking about in the ashes and smoke for a bony token of remembrance.

I needed to go home, I'd seen enough. Janet wanted to stay to watch the fire brigade arrive to extinguish the blaze, so I left her and walked back alone. The relief of cold night air quickly turned to shivering.

At home my mum was having a cup of tea, sitting on a chair in front of the fire. I wanted to talk about Tommy, but decided not to. She was listening to the radio, some quiz show in which a panel of contestants had to guess what the songs were from the first few bars. My mum was good at it. She was getting more right answers than the people on the radio. When the programme ended she turned the volume down and took her empty cup and saucer to the kitchen.

'Why does Nanny call dad a blackman?' I asked. There was no answer, only a little laugh. 'Why?' I persisted. 'Why does she always say he was black?'

My mum appeared at the kitchen door, wiping the cup with a teatowel. 'I don't know,' she said, smiling and shaking her head in bewilderment. 'She's always called him that.'

I was about to start asking some other questions when a fire-engine siren started blasting its way down Berry Street, broadcasting its arrival to the neighbourhood. I'd never witnessed the annual extinguishing of the fire, but I didn't feel like going out again. I made myself a cup of tea and got ready for bed.

Janet arrived home at about ten o'clock. She told us that before the fire engines arrived, a gang of lads had thrown a live dog onto the bonfire. And that some men, Marty Jenson and Mr Malone, had battered a couple of the lads in front of everybody. I didn't believe her. The next day the Mulhern's dog called Brownie wasn't anywhere to be found. I remembered him as a gentle, shy little mongrel with floppy velvet ears. He used to always stop by our lamppost, and as he cocked his leg he would look at me askance, almost expecting to be told off. He was never seen again.

8

Sex Appeal

Not long after her husband's death, some spirit for living 'the good life' came back into my mum. Saturday nights at the bingo were exchanged for dancehalls. In her youth during the war she had been known as a 'good-time girl' (whatever that was), but twelve years of marriage, she said, had changed her. She managed to track down Beryl, an old friend, and together they tried to recapture the excitement of the dance floor. She said dancing was a tonic, even though it had changed over the years from waltzes and foxtrots to just jigging about. She could jig about as well as anyone.

She even managed to find herself a few men friends. There was one in particular called Tony Davies. Although he was a short, fat Welshman with a large bald patch encircled by a halo of black curly tufts, my mum thought he was very attractive. He was quite taken with her, too, calling her the 'Lovely Lily'. Naturally this caused great excitement as it was a chance to acquire a new name. Janet and I hoped they would marry and he would adopt us, making us Deirdre and Janet Davies. But Cushla didn't like him and made his life a misery in any way she could. Tony tried to buy her affection with sweets, money and the promise of outings, but she remained disagreeable and surly, calling him Taffy and telling him to get back to Wales.

One evening while we were in bed, we heard my mum and Tony coming in late. They were laughing and talking for a while, then it all went quiet. Janet and I decided to sneak downstairs to find out how things were progressing. Quietly opening the door, we saw our long-legged gangly mum sitting on little fat Tony's lap. She looked like an oversized dummy sitting on an undersized ventriloquist's knee. They were kissing and his hand was up her skirt. It seemed strange to see my mum being physically affectionate and responsive to another person, murmuring with pleasure as Tony's hand probed further up her thigh. We watched them for a while before a fit of giggling beset us and we ran back to bed. I suppose their lovemaking could only take place downstairs as Cushla lay waiting in my mum's bed, as possessive as a husband.

My mum said she liked Tony because he reminded her of Mario Lanza. Although he was Welsh, he had no voice and couldn't even sing in tune. The relationship eventually ended and my mum reverted to spending Saturday nights at the bingo. Her widow's bloom hadn't even lasted a year.

My main interest in the opposite sex was still in procuring a normal surname. I knew that to attract a male required a certain amount of sex appeal. If I wanted to hook myself a man as soon as possible, he had to be lured by the right bait.

I was still flat chested with no signs of imminent womanhood. My mum said I should be enjoying childhood, and all that other stuff would come soon enough. I felt annoyed when she said things like that: it only proved how oblivious she was to our miserable state. How could anybody enjoy a childhood with the name Rammsbottom imprinted on their every moment? We were born to be ridiculed. She had been Lily Patterson, a thoroughly normal name. How dare she suggest we should try to enjoy childhood!

As I needed to ferret out the secrets of sex appeal to better my chances of an early marriage, the obvious next step was to conduct a study. I decided to survey a variety of females and assess them for sex appeal. But it was difficult to know exactly what sex appeal was. Marilyn Monroe had it, but was it her hair, her bust, her pouting lips or maybe her name? What if she had been Marilyn Rammsbottom? She could pout all she liked – people would only scoff.

It was necessary to imagine being a lad from Berry Street and observe life from that particular viewpoint. The thought of having to marry one of those spotty, obnoxious louts made me shudder, but spending all my life with the comical name was worse. Observation highlighted the fact that lads were attracted by big tits and high heels. They always whistled at certain young women who worked in the Canal Street bag factory; women who managed to swing their hips as they tottered along on their high-heeled shoes, their hair back-combed into a high roll (usually platinum blonde), and wearing a nonchalant expression. When lads whistled after them these women didn't even glance sideways at their admirers. They were used to it. This gave them an air of unavailability that only increased their sex appeal.

Continuing my assessment of local females, I knew that big tits alone weren't enough, as Pat Gawler and her huge breasts rated fairly low. I also knew a pretty face wasn't enough either; there had to be some evidence of a pair of tits. Although my mum wasn't embarrassed answering any questions we had on the subject of sex, she didn't seem knowledgeable enough to understand the subtleties of sex appeal. Some direct help was required, and who better to turn to than my old friend, Brenda Rainer. There was a girl with sex stamped on her very expression.

I invited Brenda to our house one evening to discuss the mysteries of this paradoxical subject. Brenda had grown in all directions. At fourteen she already had a womanly bust and large hips. My mum asked her if she was still earning money at the bus station, but she denied ever working there. She now had a regular boyfriend called Carl, who was one of the drummers from the Orange Lodge.

After tea Brenda came up to our room for the consultation. I allowed Janet to be present as she was in need of rescue through an early marriage just as much as I was. I wondered about having a notebook and pencil ready to jot the information down, but decided it might seem too much like school. Brenda took our interest in her sex-symbol status as a compliment. She was completely uninhibited and wasted no time in showing us her full and pendulous naked breasts.

'How did you grow them so quickly?' asked Janet, as though some sort of strong fertiliser had been involved.

'A special massage technique, like this,' explained Brenda as she kneaded her breasts in a circular motion Janet and I copied her, our hands pressed flat against our supine chests. Brenda then pulled her jersey off altogether and showed us two bushes of dark hair growing under each arm. We were impressed.

When we'd finished admiring her armpits, she went on to discuss menstruation. She explained how for a few days every month she got her period and had to wear sanitary towels. I knew what sanitary towels were because my mum kept them on the top shelf in the living room. When Janet and I first found them, we thought they were special hats and put them on our heads with the loops around both ears. There were all sorts of things on that top shelf. A thing called a Dutch cap with a box of powder. We put the powder on our faces and the only logical place for the little rubber bowl was on top of a head, like a clown might wear. We also found a condom. At the time we didn't know what it was and tried to blow it up like a balloon. The top shelf seemed to be where exciting carnival-type things were kept for a party that never took place.

Brenda continued the lesson by showing us her pubic hair. Where smooth, bare flesh had once been, there was now a dark hairy bush. We had never seen a naked adult man or woman, apart from marble statues, and they certainly didn't have pubic hair. She then talked about what boys do to girls. She told us about erections and ejaculation. I learnt more about sex from Brenda in those couple of hours than I ever did at home or school.

When the lesson was over, Brenda said goodbye to us at the front gate. As she crossed the road, a couple of men started eyeing her up and down. She turned around and smiled at us, all the time her hands were busy pulling down her jersey for the men to get a better look at her breasts, and smoothing her skirt, which accentuated the sensual movement of her hips. The men continued to stand outside our house observing Brenda, their mouths forming a whistle that never made any sound. As she walked through her own gate she gave a little wave, cocking up her back leg before disappearing into her house. Janet and I looked at each other in astonishment before closing our front door. Those men had been enchanted by Brenda and we wanted in on the magic formula.

After a fortnight of massaging my chest the way Brenda had demonstrated, the only detectable difference was a pair of aching hands. Janet had given up after a couple of days but I had persevered. Fed up waiting for nature, I decided to help myself in some other way.

Help came in the simple form of a pair of socks. Neatly rolling up the socks, I sewed them onto the inside of my vest to form a lumpy pair of breasts. With my school blouse and tunic over the vest it really seemed as though something was there. In the mirror things looked pretty authentic.

That was the top half sorted out; the bottom half was a little more difficult. My favourite doll, Irene, would have to be sacrificed, at least her hair would. The poor doll, was rigorously scalped and the dark hair, with the help of some glue, was stuck in the areas where nature had not yet progressed. I felt sticky, and all the bits and pieces felt precarious as I continued with the new image.

It was a Saturday afternoon and my mum had just left the house to go shopping. In her wardrobe there was a blue silk blouse that Tony Davies had bought her. It was sleeveless with little white pearl buttons and a round neckline. She never wore it and I don't think it would have suited her anyway, not with her breasts lying somewhere down around her waist. I quickly put it on over my vest. Tucked into a black skirt, the blouse looked quite sexy, especially with my new protrusions.

I opened the front door and stepped into the outside world to see what reactions I might encounter (this all being part of an educational study). A lad walked past as I stood at our gate but he didn't even look up at me. Mrs Gawler was at her post watching. I quickly gazed in the opposite direction, making out I was waiting for somebody rather than just nosing about. The last thing I wanted was the local lookout thinking I was setting myself up as competition.

There were a couple of men in the distance. One of them was

Mr Connor. I knew he was already married, but for research purposes I needed to observe all reactions. The men would soon be walking past our house, right past me. I quickly arranged myself in a certain posture, chest out, one hand on a hip, the other hand at the back of my head displaying Irene's matted hair under both arms. There was no way I could present my other glued scrag of hair without appearing indecent: they would have to assume. I placed one leg in front of the other to finalise the look.

It worked. The men slowed down when they saw me. Their eyes were all over my blouse as I pulled it straight for them to get a better look. 'Jesus Christ!' said Mr Connor, gawking at my body as they continued past. They both looked back at me and laughed as if I were something ridiculous. I tried to remain objective, but I felt strange, not elated as I had hoped to. I wanted to run back inside the house and hide. Hide away from men and from nature.

'What the fuck are you up to girl?' Mrs Gawler asked in her usual straightforward manner, looking me up and down the way the women in the shop had looked at Brenda.

'Nothink,' I replied as I headed towards Brenda's house. I could feel her eyes on my back as I strutted across the road. The doll's hair inside my knickers was making me itchy and I couldn't help but have a quick scratch as I knocked on the Rainers' door. Mrs Rainer opened and I asked if Brenda was in. I was glad it was her and not her husband. She didn't seem to recognise me and called to Brenda that there was somebody for her. I straightened the blouse again, hoping Brenda would notice my new figure, but when she came to the door she said hello and didn't seem to notice anything different about me.

'Look, I've got a bust,' I pointed out to her. 'And some hairs.' I lifted my arms up for her to view the evidence. There was an unexpected silence while Brenda observed the new me.

'You're all wonky' she said pointing at my blouse. One sock had managed to roll down, creating an instant mastectomy. She also told me that one lot of underarm hair was sticking to the blouse rather than to my left armpit. My face boiled hot with embarrassment. I turned to go, saying thanks to Brenda for letting me know, and that it had only been a joke.

Back home I snapped the cotton holding the socks to the vest and winced as I pulled the hair away from my body. Poor baldy Irene was still sitting on the bed where I'd left her, smiling her silly doll's smile. I hung my mum's blouse back in her wardrobe and then did what most women do when things go wrong. I made myself a cup of tea.

Feeling a combination of shame and anger, I reminded myself that this was a fact-gathering study; it was first-hand information that had been gained the hard way. In my notebook I wrote: Tits must be real.

The front door was opening. It was my mum and sisters back from shopping. 'What've you been doin'?' Janet asked. She always seemed to know when I'd been up to something.

'Nothink,' I answered, suddenly remembering that the left underarm hair was still stuck to my mum's blouse in the wardrobe. 'Nothink,' I repeated.

9

The Friends

There was an old red-brick church on Stanley Road. Outside the door a large sign read 'A cordial welcome guaranteed!' One Sunday when my friend Valerie and I were passing, we read the sign and decided to have a look inside. A couple of expensive-type cars were parked in the church grounds. We tested their doors to see if they were locked, and they were. Even though the front door of the church was wide open, inside was dark and empty and smelt of musty clothes. Hardly a cordial welcome.

We wandered about in the pews, picking up hymn books and putting them down again. The old inclination to look for money on the floor came over me. I never did get over the thrill of finding that half-crown on the bus floor, and although it was some years before, I still lived in hope of another such find.

But the floors were completely bare, not even a sweet wrapper to be found. There was a huge organ by the altar with a large open music book. I pressed one of the black keys and it made a sombre, echoing sound. We started to laugh and pressed a few more keys. Suddenly a very tall, completely bald, elderly man appeared. His head stretched forward from an old crumpled neck, reminding me of a tortoise sticking its head out of its shell. 'Good afternoon young ladies,' he said in a deep voice, his hand extended ready for us to shake. We jumped down from the organ and I shook the hand. It was a large cold hand with a surprising amount of strength in it for an old man. Valerie also shook his hand. 'Come and meet the rest of us' the man said, turning towards a door at the back of the church and beckoning us to follow. We clambered down some stone stairs towards a lighted area which seemed to be underneath the church.

'He's gonna murder us,' I whispered to Valerie, but she only laughed.

The tall man opened a door and invited us into a large, windowless room containing a semicircle of seated people at one end. They were assembled around a small electric heater. As we entered, they stopped talking and looked up. Most of them were old women wearing hats and smiling vacantly. One of them put her book down and scuttled towards us.

'My, what have we here? Two little girls!' she said smiling and studying us as though we were from another world. Her voice was as high as the bald man's was low.

'They were playing the organ upstairs,' explained the bald man, his teeth bared in what was probably a smile.

'Playing the organ!' The woman seemed on the verge of hysteria as she clapped her chubby little hands together and started laughing in a high-pitched squeal.

'Well, we're very, very pleased to meet you,' she said, shaking our hands vigorously. 'My name is Aunty Lena and this is Mr Hulzt.'

Valerie and I nodded politely. Aunty Lena reminded me of one of those people who never outgrow the Girl Guides. She didn't have a Liverpudlian accent like us. Her voice sounded as though she had known privilege and elocution.

'And all these people here,' she said, her outstretched arm

indicating the others still sitting, 'these are The Friends.' The Friends smiled without getting up. Valerie looked at me and I knew what she was thinking. Should we make a run for the door?

'And what's your name dear?' Aunty Lena was asking Valerie. This sort of question always caused my heart to beat faster.

'Valerie Wilson.'

'Valerie!' repeated Aunty Lena. 'How wonderful!' She turned towards me with her pumpkin-smiling face. 'And what's your name lovey?'

I wanted to make a name up. Sometimes I'd say Deirdre Robertson, but Valerie knew my real name so I couldn't get away with that here. 'I'm Deirdre,' I said, hoping that would suffice.

'What a wonderful name!' she gushed. 'Deirdre.'

It was obvious that everything was going to be wonderful for this excitable little woman. For the moment I seemed to have been spared the embarrassment of having to say my full name. We were then ushered over to The Friends and introduced to them one at a time, shaking their feeble hands and putting up with their bad breath and smiling, nodding heads. We were certainly being given the promised cordial welcome.

On closer inspection, one or two of The Friends weren't so physically old, but their manners were. One of them, called Alice, who had a face like an apple pudding that had been left to go hairy, asked us if we were sisters. I was about to say yes, but Valerie was already telling them no. After a little lecture from Aunty Lena on how the Lord had directed us to the church and how there must be a reason – 'all to the glory of His great name' – she insisted on us coming again next Sunday at one o'clock for the Sunday school lesson.

Outside on Stanley Road the air seemed fresh and sweet compared to the jumble-sale stink inside the church. Valerie and

I decided they were all senile and we definitely wouldn't be going back the following week.

I was secretly quite pleased that somebody had thought Deirdre a wonderful name, even if she was only a little religious maniac. So the following Sunday I persuaded Janet to come along to the Sunday school with me. Just before one o'clock we opened the church door, but this time it wasn't empty. In the pews people had their heads bowed and Mr Hulzt was standing at the front giving a sermon. He was behind a lectern and his deep voice echoed through the stale air.

As the door creaked, they all looked around. Mr Hulzt continued in his monotonous tone as another bald man hobbled towards us. He limped up to us and asked what we wanted. I said we had come for the Sunday school. The man, who I'd not met before, had a kind face with intelligent brown eyes. He asked us to wait outside and Aunty Lena would come and fetch us when the service was over.

After a short time Aunty Lena appeared, waving at us in her lively manner. 'Deirdre, how wonderful of you to come!' She seemed to have a good memory for names.

'This is my sister Janet,' I said, pushing Janet forward for inspection.

'You brought your sister, how wonderful,' she said, her eyes screwing up as she said the word sist-er. She liked to put special emphasis on certain words by saying them deliberately slowly and screwing up her eyes at the same time. This was probably to show how sincere her feelings were on that subject.

'You know lovey, it was Andrew who brought his broth-er, Simon Peter, to meet Jesus,' she informed us, shaking hands with Janet like a keen salesman meeting a new customer.

We followed Aunty Lena to the entrance at the back where the

A Dandelion By Any Other Name

Sunday school was held. Walking down a different lot of stone steps we entered the familiar room below. Another old woman, a tall, thin woman called Aunty Phyllis, appeared and provided us with yet another cordial welcome. Both women wore hats, even though they had removed their coats. After a few minutes, two blond little boys arrived. They were called Stephen and James and were the sons of one of The Friends. The boys spoke with aristocratic voices and took hardly any notice of us.

I was surprised that the six of us – two sisters, two brothers and two old ladies – made up the entire Sunday school. We sat in a little circle around an electric heater, even though it wasn't turned on. Aunty Lena commenced with a short prayer, thanking God for bringing us together and then we sang a hymn called 'The Beauty of Jesus' while Aunty Phyllis played the piano. The only audible voices belonged to the two women – shrill, warbling and slightly off key. They tried to make up for the musical deficiency by smiling toothy smiles as they sang. Janet and I didn't know the hymn and the two boys were more intent on kicking each other with their nicely polished black shoes than joining in the singing.

We were then given a Bible each and asked to read a couple of lines from Isaiah, Chapter 53. Aunty Lena then went on and on about having to take the consequences for our actions. I couldn't see any relevance between the verses in the old testament and her lecture. The session concluded in a final prayer. James and Stephen were still kicking each other all the way through Aunty Lena's lengthy closing prayer, while Aunty Phyllis indicated with a wagging forefinger that they were to behave themselves. The boys totally ignored her. Janet whispered that she was bored and wanted to go home. At three o'clock on the dot, we all echoed our amens and the ordeal was declared over.

'Now Uncle Donald has kindly donated some more chocolate

for the Sunday school children,' said Aunty Lena, as she unwrapped a large brown paper bag. The contents of the bag were a greedy child's dream. Dozens of bars of chocolate. Janet's eyes reflected my own as they lit up with astonishment, gazing at the treasure trove before us. We were each given six large bars of milk chocolate. Apparently this Uncle Donald worked in a chocolate factory and each week he brought a bag of seconds for the Sunday school children. James and Stephen didn't seem to mind sharing the chocolate with us. I suppose they had become sick of it, but Janet and I knew we were onto a winner.

'Oh thank, you Arnt Lena,' I said, feigning the posh accent of the two blond thoroughbreds. The twelve bars of chocolate were quickly secured in our pockets, and after promising we would definitely come again next week, we ran like two wild horses all the way home, down Trinity Road, past the public baths and through the subway tunnel into Berry Street. It was a quarter-past three on the Bootle Town Hall clock as we bolted upstairs to inspect our chocolate bonanza in the quiet of the bedroom. Cushla, suspecting something was going on, burst into the room and saw the twelve bars spread out over the bed. We told her she was only allowed one bite and that if she wanted the same copious amount, she would have to come to Sunday school next week.

By Tuesday evening all the chocolate had been devoured. Calculations for chocolate bars were drawn up for months into the future. We even conjured up ways of getting rid of the two blond boys so as to secure their share of the chocolate. But on the following Sunday we were disappointed to find that a whole family of Murphys were also members of the Sunday school and had turned up for the session. No doubt rapacious Catholics anxious to get in on the free handouts.

The prayers and tedious Bible readings went on and on. At last the hands of the clock on the wall were pointing to three o'clock – Chocolate Time. Following a hearty amen, Aunty Lena opened the brown paper bag, and calculated we would only receive two bars each because of the number of the Murphy children present. I observed the Murphys: how they pocketed their share of the chocolate with the enthusiasm of the deprived. The blond boys with the la-de-da voices didn't seem particularly upset, even though they had now dropped from six to two bars in one week.

There were eight Murphys, ranging from Maureen, who was sixteen, down to little Jimmy, who was only two. I suppose they were really quite an attractive family, but we saw them only as chocolate grabbers. They all had jet-black straight hair and blue eyes. Aunty Lena seemed to be particularly fond of Maureen and made a great fuss of her. All the Murphys were clean and tidy and even bragged about how they washed their feet every night.

'Ours don't get that dirty,' I said looking at Janet, knowing how grimy, especially between the toes, our feet could be.

'Cleanliness is next to godliness,' declared Maureen, closing her Bible and putting an end to the discussion.

Over the following weeks Janet and I expressed our contempt for the Murphys subtly, by not smiling at them or socialising with them. When little Jimmy started whimpering during prayers, I frowned sanctimoniously at the struggling child on Maureen's knee, then turned to Aunty Phyllis, silently pleading for some human if not divine intervention. Aunty Phyllis fussed about like a mime artist, putting her finger over her lips in an exaggerated manner, hovering over little Jimmy and finally hunching her shoulders at the futility of her efforts while Aunty Lena, with tightly closed eyes, beseeched Heavenly Father to bless us and make us tools for His glory.

At home, Janet and I discussed the Murphy problem. There

seemed to be only one line of action to take, and that was to physically meet this Uncle Donald who worked at the chocolate factory, and get ourselves well in with him. The following Sunday I asked Aunty Lena if we could thank Uncle Donald in person for all his kindness to us. She said that if we wanted to meet Donald we would have to stay for the evening service. He was one of The Friends who only made an appearance at about six o'clock. I told her I would very much like to stay, but Janet didn't want to.

At three o'clock Janet went off home with her share of the chocolate while I hung about the church. Aunty Phyllis made a pot of tea in the little kitchen just off the large room and Mr Hulzt and the lame man joined us for afternoon tea. I learned that Mr Hulzt was Aunty Lena's husband and that the lame man, James Riding, was married to Aunty Phyllis. There was also a woman called Gladys there, who was the mother of the boys, James and Stephen. She was a mousy little Welsh woman with dark hair and dark eyes, nothing like her Aryan-looking sons. The boys had spent some time at a boarding school which is how they acquired their fancy way of speaking.

We were eating homemade wholemeal scones with our cups of tea. They called the scones 'scoans'. I'd never heard them called that and I wished Janet were next to me so I could have a secret giggle with her.

'Would you like another scone, Mr Hulzt?' Aunty Lena asked her husband in her high-pitched voice.

'No thank you, Aunty Lena.'

At about four o'clock, some more of The Friends arrived for a Bible study. There was Hairy Alice Pudding; Isabelle, who had appalling breath; a very old man, who could hardly see or hear, called Brother Burrows; Roy Garston, who owned a little fruit and veg shop in Crosby; and George Grey, who Aunty Lena described as 'a lovely boy'. George was over fifty, a bachelor with mad, staring eyes. He looked after his elderly mother. 'You know lovey,' Aunty Lena said, 'you can always judge a man by the way he treats his moth-er.' George the lovely boy looked a bit psychotic to me, but then Grey was a normal name. Deirdre Grey sounded fine.

The hour of Bible study seemed insufferably long. Some of the people, especially Mr Hulzt and Isabelle, acted as though they were part of an amateur dramatic group, raising and lowering their voices for effect and saying amen (pronounced ay-men) after almost everything. I wondered if they said amen instead of excuse me when they farted. When it finally ended, the kettle was put on again for more tea. Cucumber sandwiches and fruit cake were served over an extended table.

I became the centre of attention. People were asking me all sorts of questions and at last the inevitable question came. 'And what's your family name lovey?' It was Aunty Lena's voice, her eyes scrutinising mine, waiting for the answer. I thought of lying and saying Robertson, but as I was inside a church I decided to tell the truth. But when I spoke I could only say Ramms. The bottom stuck in my throat and wouldn't come out.

'Ramms! Oh my, what an unusual name.' A few seconds after speaking, I tried to complete the name but it was too late. They had seized upon the peculiarity of the name Ramms and were testing out the sound and guessing at its origins.

'It's an Egyptian name,' said Aunty Phyllis.

'No Phyllis dear, you're thinking of Ramses,' Aunty Lena explained. 'Ramms is of Dutch extraction, isn't that right, lovey?'

'I think so,' I said, hoping they would change the subject.

'Is your father Dutch?' asked James Riding, pouring himself another cup of tea.

'He's dead,' I said with a solemn expression, bowing my head as though the subject were very painful for me. That immediately stopped the questions about the name. Alice offered me more cake, but I'd already had three pieces and declined a fourth.

Before the evening service, Aunty Lena asked me to have a little walk outside the church with her. She opened the big shiny Rover car door to put the remains of her food away. In the back window of the car was a large Bible with gold-edged pages. 'How many brothers and sisters do you have, Deirdre?' she asked, pulling at the car door to make sure it was properly locked.

'Two sisters and a brother,' I answered.

'How wonderful for your moth-er.' I couldn't fathom what she meant. My mum didn't seem to associate motherhood with anything wonderful.

'You know, Deirdre, God has chosen you to do a special job for His glory.' A pause followed, my cue to inquire after the Special Job but I remained silent. Just then, a car pulled up outside and a man carrying a Bible and a large paper bag appeared. 'Brother Donald!'

The man was in his forties, with red tufts of hair around a medium-sized bald patch. I was introduced and said thank you to him for all the chocolate he had given us. He seemed quite shy and blushed when I mentioned it. I'd never seen a man blush before and it made me feel as awkward as he did. He passed the paper bag to Aunty Lena saying it was for next week's Sunday school.

Inside the church some of The Friends were settled in the pews for the evening service. Gladys was fussing with some flowers at the front and Brother James was walking towards the organ. One of his legs wouldn't bend, so with the help of a cane, he managed to swing himself about. He looked like a stick insect, with lots of legs all going in different directions. Mr Hulzt was to give the sermon and he was already standing before the lectern, his shiny head buried in a Bible and a pile of papers.

The service commenced with a sombre piece of organ music. The sound of the organ in the empty church made me feel strange. I wanted to cry. It sounded familiar, as if it were evoking something that had been part of my life a long, long time ago. But I'd never been in a church before, except when I was christened. I stood up without any explanation and quickly left the church and the evocative music.

While hurrying along Trinity Road, a car slowed down beside me. It was Donald. 'Are you all right, love?' he shouted from the window. His accent was the same as ours, not like some of the others with their pedigree voices.

'Yeah,' I nodded. 'I was feelin' sick.'

'Would yer like a lift home?' I knew I wasn't supposed to accept lifts from strange men, but Donald had been introduced to me, so I said yes.

The only other car I'd ever been in was at my dad's funeral, so it was a great novelty to climb into the front passenger seat of Donald's white Escort. It smelt of polish. I glanced at the back seat but there was no sign of any more chocolate.

'Where d'you live, love?'

'Berry Street.' I could see from his expression that he didn't know where that was, so I explained if he turned right into Balliol Road he could get there that way. He asked me if all the chocolate from the Sunday school had made me sick, so I quickly said no. That was the last thing I wanted him thinking. I explained it was the organ in the church. It had frightened me in some way and made me feel sick. Donald promised that if I came next week he would sit next to me throughout the service to make sure I didn't get frightened. I agreed to his suggestion. He must have felt awkward again, as his face started to go as red as his hair.

'Are yer married?' I asked, trying to be conversational. He snorted a laugh and said he wasn't. 'What's yer surname then?' I asked, looking at the red curly hair and imagining angelic little red-haired daughters.

'What is this? Twenty questions or something?' he said, glancing sideways at me. I remembered I was supposed to be sick and quickly put my hand on my brow as we turned into Berry Street. I asked if I could get out at the corner because of nosy Mrs Gawler. Before I left I said thank you yet again for the Sunday school chocolate. He said he'd try to get some extra stuff from the factory for me next week.

I had done it! From now on the Murphys wouldn't be in the same league. As soon as Donald's car was out of sight I ran home full of high spirits, and told Janet of my triumph. She agreed to accompany me to the evening service the following week. Even Cushla wanted to come. Cushy could tell when there was something big happening. On the table my piece of chocolate cake awaited, but I offered it to Cushla. 'For yer spindly legs.' There was nothing like the glow of success to make a person feel magnanimous. Janet wanted to know what Donald's surname was. I told her we'd find out next week by writing him a special thank you for the chocolate.

All week we talked about Donald, imagining how great it would be working in a chocolate factory. He would probably help get us a job there when we left school. Being at a 'girls only' secondary school, there was little contact with males apart from the Berry Street louts. Donald had a car, he was unmarried, he was kind, and he could bring home the chocolate. And he probably had a normal surname – most people did. Oh yes, Donald certainly had potential.

A Dandelion By Any Other Name

I asked Cushla and Tommy to come to the next Sunday school lesson, improving the chocolate ratio a bit in our favour. Cushla promised to come but Tommy wasn't interested. He had started work as a delivery boy for a large bakery firm and we didn't see much of him. Being a Catholic, he didn't want to go inside any church other than his own Saint James.

Cushla was seven years old and not shy in the way Janet and I had been. She had long blond hair and large blue eyes with thick eyelashes. The deformity of the surname had not yet afflicted her the way it had me. She seemed to know it was only a temporary situation and looked on her world, small though it was, as a squire's eldest son might look on his future estate.

Aunty Lena greeted Cushla with the usual fuss. How wonderful everything was. Three sisters all finding their way to God. I could tell Cushla didn't like being stroked or squeezed by Aunty Lena. Her bottom lip was starting to pout, a sure signal she was becoming annoyed, the way a cat moves its tail in anger before it scratches.

I'd seen that lip before at the Immunisation Centre a few months earlier. A nurse was trying to distract Cushla's attention away from a vaccination needle by being overly friendly. Cushla had yelled 'Bitch!' when the needle made contact with her arm.

'That's not a very nice word for a little girl to use,' said the surprised nurse, dabbing the arm with cotton wool. To prove how nice Cushy really was, a barrage of obscenities shot from her sweet, heart-shaped mouth. Nasty words such as shit, fuck, dickarse (her favourite), piss and bugger. My mum started grinning with embarrassment and quickly took her youngest daughter outside. Janet and I were so impressed by our little sister's performance that hours later that same day we were still imitating the unfortunate scene.

But now the lip was protruding again, and Cushla's repertoire of rude words was the last thing I wanted Aunty Lena to hear. I remembered what was in my pocket – a hat. It was a navy-blue beret which I quickly put on my head to distract Cushla. But I had brought it specifically to look like one of The Friends, to be a member of their special club. Aunty Lena noticed the hat and was beside herself with praise for me. Take that Maureen Murphy, I thought.

Aunty Phyllis clucked about like an old hen, wanting to know who Cushla was. 'This is little Cushla Ramms, Deirdre and Janet's younger sister,' said Aunty Lena.

'Bottom!' said Cushla with an angry look. I was horrified and frowned at Janet, who had started giggling. Cushla immediately twigged that she was holding some sort of power.

'What's that, lovey?' said Aunty Lena, pushing her ear into Cushla's face.

'Rammsbottom! You missed the Bottom,' explained Cushla.

Aunty Lena was bewildered and just laughed her throaty laugh as though a joke had been told that she hadn't got. But Aunty Phyllis, with her excellent hearing, had got it. She shot me an accusing look. I quickly ordered Janet to take Cushla home. She was too dangerous to have loose in a Sunday school, especially with the squeaky clean Murphys about to arrive. I ushered them both out telling Aunty Lena that Cushla didn't feel well, but Janet would come back later. My capacity for lying disturbed me, but behind all my sins lay the unfortunate name.

Distant cries about chocolate could be heard as Janet dragged our bellowing little sister out of the church. 'Oh my!' said Aunty Lena.

In the middle of the Bible lesson Janet reappeared. She passed me a little note saying I looked stupid sitting about in a hat. But stupid or not, I was gaining points. I was the one asked to close in prayer, a privilege that even Maureen, as far as I was aware, had never been granted. I parroted one of Aunty Lena's prayers, and I could tell she was inwardly beaming behind her tightly closed eyes. Looking about during the prayer it seemed Aunty Lena was the only one taking it seriously. Even Aunty Phyllis was busy studying the contents of her delicately embroidered hanky.

An emotional encore of amens burst from Aunty Lena's lips when I finished, and she gave me a special lingering look when she opened her beady brown eyes. I was the Chosen One all right. The chocolate was divided in the usual way, then a stampede of children raced to the door for home.

Somehow we managed to get through the afternoon Bible study and tea. My hat was greatly admired by The Friends and was even mentioned in a prayer. It was the principle they applauded. If I'd been wearing a tea cosy on my head, they would have approved.

'You're stuck with that now,' said Janet, looking at the beret.

'You'll have to wear one next week,' I whispered. 'It's compulsory.'

'Never!'

The female Friends wore hats because the Bible said it was a sin for a woman to have a bare head in church. I looked at Mr Hulzt's completely bald head and wondered why he could get away with it. Surely his hairless head was more offensive to God than a good female head of hair? 'Faith,' Aunty Lena would beam, when I asked such questions. 'We don't question God lovey, not ever!'

So we began asking questions about Donald instead. We discovered his surname was Campbell. It sounded a bit Scottish, so in our imaginings we had him doing what Scottish people do – twirling about in a kilt and throwing logs into the air. Deirdre

Campbell had a good sound to it. What a new wee image that would be! We also wanted to know where he lived. How old was he? What exactly did he do at the chocolate factory? 'My, you're very interested in Brother Donald today,' noted Aunty Lena. 'He's a lovely boy, very good to his moth-er, just like Brother George.' On hearing his name mentioned, Brother George smiled his psychotic smile, while old Brother Burrows bumbled about, putting hymn books he could barely see into pews he kept bumping into. That seemed to be his little job each week and kept him happily occupied.

At last Donald arrived, but we were disappointed to see he only carried a Bible. He wore a grey raincoat, the same one he had on the previous week. Janet simpered when I introduced her to him, making a movement that resembled something between a bow and a curtsy. He told Janet that the Scottish version of her name was Jean. She seemed to like that, and said we could call her Jean instead of Janet. Any talk of names made me nervous so I quickly changed the subject and asked Donald if he had ever been in love. 'Only with the Lord,' he answered after the initial shock of the question, his face and neck reddening.

During the evening service Janet and I sat on either side of Donald. I tried to listen for his voice during the singing but he must have been miming because there was no sound coming out. Aunty Lena was standing in front of us and she stretched up on her toes and back down again. She did this repetitively as she sang in her shrill, tuneless voice. She could really murder a hymn. I caught Janet's eye so she could watch me stretch up and down on my toes as Aunty Lena did. Soon Janet started doing it too, the three of us in unison. There was nobody behind us, so only Donald could observe our antics. He smiled nervously and carried on miming.

A Dandelion By Any Other Name

Mr Hulzt was giving the sermon. It was difficult to concentrate on his words as there were so many unusual people to distract us. Entertainment was everywhere. Old Mr Burrows looked a bit worried. With his eyes tightly closed, he fiddled about with his hearing aid, straining to hear the sermon or to switch it out – it was hard to know which.

The gist of the sermon was this: if you're happy in life, there is something wrong. The follower of Christ should not be happy. There should always be problems and pain. It all sounded like a great philosophy to live by. He talked of the Second Coming, how it will be like a thief in the night. The unhappy followers of Christ will rise up to be with God in His glory, while those who found happiness in this worldly life will be sent to some dark place for punishment. He didn't say where it was.

When the joyful message was finally over, Janet and I walked about shaking hands with The Friends, saying goodbye to them. Janet was shaking Mr Burrows' hand but he didn't seem to know who she was and couldn't hear her. Donald came to the rescue. 'Brother Burrows, it's Jean!' he shouted down the old man's ear.

'Jesus?' inquired the old man.

Janet and I giggled. The trembling withered hand was still holding onto hers, shaking away wildly.

'Jean! The sister of Deirdre, she's saying goodbye to you,' explained Donald, raising his eyes in mock frustration. I could see he was starting to feel embarrassed at having to yell, especially calling Janet by a different name. A pet name. Poor Brother Burrows let go of Janet's hand. He looked quite relieved to find it wasn't quite yet the Second Coming.

As we left the church I gave Donald the note I'd written saying thank you very much for the chocolate. It was a pathetic gesture, but he seemed moved by it and said he had managed to bring some extras for us. After giving Aunty Lena the regular Sunday school bag, he asked us if we'd like a lift home as it was raining. We jumped eagerly into the car. I sat in the front with Donald while Janet sat behind. On the back seat lay a brown paper bag. It was the promised extra chocolate, and we were to let him know if there were any more special bars we might like. Janet fingered the bag, but I quickly pulled it from her and thanked Donald profusely. I didn't like to look inside it while he was there. I wanted to appear grateful, not greedy.

We were dropped off outside our house. The rain had obviously driven Mrs Gawler inside as there was nobody to see us climbing out of the car. We said goodbye to Donald and rushed inside with the goods, scattering the contents all over the floor in the living room. There were all sorts of different chocolate bars, the types of chocolate we saw in the shops but never dreamed of buying for ourselves.

That evening a vicious fight erupted between Janet and me over the chocolate. She pulled my hair and I scratched and pinched her arms. My mum intervened, saying she was going to tell that bloody Sunday school teacher not to give us any more chocolate. 'Yer like friggin' animals over a carcass!'

That stopped us. I suddenly thought of my dad. How he used to come home on a Friday night with a bag of chocolate for us. How we almost mugged him to get at the bag. Yes, we were like animals. Selfish peevish bitches. And chocolate was about to be reborn as the new currency used in exchange for attention and affection. A token of power. And like absolute power, chocolate would corrupt absolutely!

10

A Pervert

Over time Donald became a special friend, taking Janet and me home from church every Sunday evening in his car. We talked about him often, imagining what he might look like with no clothes on. On Saturdays he took us on outings to North Wales or to the stony beach at Morcombe, where we would stroll and talk for hours. Donald walked between us, his hands always in his pockets, the three of us discussing everything from pop music to the theory of evolution.

The amount of chocolate we consumed was incredible. And what was even more incredible was the fact that we never became fat or spotty. Truckloads of chocolate were consumed. All Donald's wages must have been spent buying 'seconds' from the factory as our appetite for chocolate was insatiable.

Donald's interest in us had not gone unnoticed by Mrs Gawler. 'A man his age shouldn't be hangin' about with them young girls!' she warned my mum.

'He's from the church,' my mum assured her.

'Church or no fuckin' church, yer shouldn't be lettin' them go off with him. He's a fuckin' pervert, wearin' that mac all through summer and winter.'

My mum steered us into the house before an argument developed. She didn't like to involve herself with the women in the street. Janet asked what a pervert was. 'It's a dirty old man,' I explained, 'like them men in the park who pull their mickeys out. A flasher.'

Mrs Gawler's warning must have been noted, as on the next outing with Donald, my mum asked if she and Cushla could come too. So on a fine Saturday morning in July, the five of us set off for Southport. My mum sat in the front with Donald while her three girls occupied the back seat. Normally he would chatter away, asking us all sorts of questions and even taping our answers on his recorder. But with my mum there he seemed quiet and sensible. Ever since Mrs Gawler accused him of being a pervert I observed him carefully. I tried to get a glimpse under his raincoat, but he always had it well fastened up. I wasn't sure what I expected to see other than a pair of trousers.

In Southport we had dinner in a little cafe. A slovenly old waitress in slippers shuffled back and forward with the orders. I noticed Donald didn't eat anything but insisted on paying the bill. My mum ordered an apple pie, which was as hard as a brick. She banged it repeatedly with her spoon to demonstrate its concrete-like texture, complaining loudly for the waitress to hear. She was also blaspheming. I felt embarrassed, knowing Donald would be offended.

After dinner we ventured into the fairground. Once again it was Donald paying for everything. There was a thing called the Mad House, where you had to walk your way through obstacles that were moving. My mum hated it. 'Ah shite!' she called, followed by the usual 'Purgatory!' as she wasn't able to make any progress towards the exit. Donald offered her his arm, escorting her out of the hellish place. 'Jesus!' she said, 'they should be paying us to go in there.' Her voice was extra loud for the benefit of the fairground attendant, a spotty lad who totally ignored her.

The next ride we went on was the Waltzes. Cushla and my mum went in one waltzer car while Donald, Janet and I sat in another. When the violent spinning round and round started, Janet's dress was caught by the wind and blew up revealing her shabby knickers. She was screaming and laughing, not daring to let go a hand to cover herself. I wished she had chosen better knickers, not those old grey-white things with broken elastic. Luckily I was wearing sensible trousers.

I made two observations during the few minutes we were riding in the waltzers. Firstly, Donald couldn't take his eyes away from Janet's uncovered legs and knickers. The word 'pervert' was on my mind and I wanted to yell it at him. The second observation was that my mum and Cushla were both hating the ride. There was a panic-stricken expression on both their faces. My mum was mouthing 'Purgatory', but the loud music drowned out her distress call. When the waltzer cars finally stopped, Cushla was crying as she'd banged her head, and my mum was dizzy and feeling sick. Although it was only half-past one, we all had to go home.

In the car on the way back nobody spoke. The silence seemed to blame Donald for the day's misfortunes. The hard apple pie, the traumatic experience on the rides, Janet's knicker display. The radio was turned on to blot out the awkward quiet. Janet was sitting in the middle on the back seat. Again, I noticed Donald. He was pretending to look in his rear mirror at the traffic behind, but it was Janet's legs he was really trying to see.

'He's lookin' up yer frock,' I whispered to Janet. She immediately pulled her dress down and clamped her legs together. I glared accusingly at Donald to show I'd twigged to his game. He quickly readjusted the rear mirror and pretended to wonder if we were on the right road. It was the one and only main road from Southport to Liverpool, so he must have been feeling guilty to ask such a foolish question.

When he dropped us off home, my mum asked him if he'd like a cup of tea before driving back to Seaforth where he lived. 'No thanks Mrs Rammsbottom,' he said. 'I'd better be gettin' off.'

He said our name! I wondered how he managed to find it out, as I'd been very careful never to mention it. He was trying to raise himself up a little by putting us down. That was all anybody needed to do to put us down: simply say the name. We let him drive off without the usual fuss of thanking him.

'He is a pervert!' I declared. 'I caught him lookin' up her frock in the car, and he only took us on the waltzers so he could ogle at her knickers.'

'Oh Jesus, don't mention them waltzers,' said my mum, placing her hand across her brow. 'Never again!'

As Janet and I grew into our teens we continued to attend the church, mainly for the free chocolate. Old Mr Burrows died, leaving us as sole representatives of the poor working class. The Friends (or Fiends, as we now called them) began to make nuisances of themselves. Every one of them (apart from Donald) could be described as well-to-do, middle-class types, living in areas such as Allerton and Formby, but wanting to emulate the humble Christ by having their church in Bootle. Being based in Bootle gave them opportunities to associate with the working-class sinners of the world such as Janet and me. There were extra points to be scored in heaven for such associations, and I suppose we were the only obvious candidates.

Every Thursday after school the shiny Rover would be parked

outside our house. Berry Street kids gaped in wonder, while Mrs Gawler positively bristled with the intrusion of it all. Aunty Lena came to show us how to sew dishcloths while Mr Hulzt tried to teach us to play hymns on an old piano they had installed in our front parlour. He had given up on Janet, as she was unable to make any sort of musical progress, but he thought I was the next Clara Schumann. I could play the hymns by ear and from memory, but I couldn't read a note of the music placed before me. Aunty Lena clapped her little fat hands together with joy when I finished 'Onward Christian Soldiers'. I'd been pretending to read the notes from the sheet, looking studiously at all the squiggly lines on the page.

'What a wonderful teacher you are, Mr Hulzt,' she cried.

'It's not me, Aunty Lena, it's the Lord working through this young lady.' He put his huge cold hand on my shoulder. His fingers were as big as carrots.

The cartoon *Popeye the Sailor* was on in the living room and I was aching to go and watch it. Janet had finished her dishcloth and while the Hulzts were absorbed in my piano playing she sneaked away to watch TV. Before they went home they liked to finish with a prayer. Janet, my mum and Cushla were called into the parlour to be part of it. My mum sometimes laughed when they drove off, calling them poor old things.

Aunty Phyllis was always bringing us bags of old clothes. They stunk of mothballs and were the types of dresses that only old women wore. We feigned great pleasure in receiving such charity, pretending to admire the baggy floral size 16 dresses with buckle belts. 'Wow, thank you, Aunty Phyllis,' I fawned, holding one of the ridiculous dresses against my thin body. I was becoming such a sycophantic hypocrite, the sound of my own words made me angry. Janet was struggling not to giggle at the sight of the baggy dark-green dress with white and yellow spots. I was annoyed at the thought – or rather the lack of thought – that went into their Christian help. I wanted to say: What exactly do you think we are, giving us these sorts of clothes? Can't you see we'd look like mongols if we wore them?

The moment Aunty Phyllis left our house, her face alight with the thoughts of good deeds and greediness for the comforts of heaven, we bundled the clothes into a pillow slip and set off for the Berry Street Rag Yard. We sometimes got three shillings for the bundle. They had good quality labels – 'pure lamb's wool'. Expensive clothes, but unwearable.

Donald continued to bring us chocolate, but we became increasingly belligerent towards him. When he took us out in his car Janet and I would sit in the back and throw rolled-up sweet wrappers at his bald spot. He knew we were treating him with contempt, but our company seemed more important to him than his own self-esteem. No amount of chocolate appeased our increasing hostility.

He continued to remain particularly fond of Janet, or Jean as he preferred to call her. One day he even hinted that he was waiting for her to grow up, that the Lord Himself had promised she would be his future wife. Janet wasn't afraid of Donald. She was quite flattered that anybody would want her, and of course there was the issue of the new surname. Even my mum said she could do a lot worse than him, overlooking the fact that he was in his mid-forties.

I enjoyed telling nasty tales to Aunty Lena; sordid details about the drunken louts hanging about outside pubs in Bootle, swearing and taking the Lord's name in vain. She was easily shocked, and consoled me in the fact that the Second Coming was nigh and these sinners would be deeply ashamed of themselves on that

Wonderful Day. 'How dreadful!' she cried, when I told her of Donald's claim to Janet as his child-bride, sanctioned by the Lord. 'Donald is very wrong to say those sorts of things to a thirteen-year-old girl. Very wrong.' She would have a word with Mr Hulzt and after praying for guidance they'd decide what should be done. I felt triumphant. Donald would be dealt with; not only for perving after young girls but for having the audacity to prefer Janet over me. It was too bad about the chocolate, but sometimes sacrifices have to be made.

I watched and waited, but nothing happened. Donald turned up for the evening service and gave us a lift home afterwards. If he had been told off it didn't seem to have had any effect on him. I was disappointed.

The following Sunday, Janet and I were secretly giggling away as usual throughout the evening service. A snot on the end of Brother George's nose had caught our attention and set us off in that hot exhausting suppressed laughter that fills the eyes with tears and twists at the insides. Donald was sitting next to us and was always amused by our giggling. Suddenly Janet's strangled laughter escaped. What should have been a quiet intake of breath turned into a loud snort. Everybody turned round and we were revealed for what we really were – sacrilegious. Mr Hulzt stopped in the middle of his sermon and stared at us. Judgement Day had come. I put my hand over my eyes in an effort to look as though I was praying rather than laughing. Janet was not so prudent, she giggled openly and uncontrollably before all the disappointed faces of The Friends. Even when the congregation returned their attention towards the front, Mr Hulzt couldn't continue his sermon.

'Young people of our fellowship,' he said, gazing at us over his horn-rimmed glasses.

'Here we go,' said Donald under his breath, as though a man of his age came into that category.

'It is an abomination,' continued the big man up front, 'to have this sort of behaviour in the house of the Lord.' Mr Hulzt blazed his cold blue eyes at us. If eyes really are the mirror of the soul, then he was the one in trouble. The sight of his lumpy shiny head and straight stern line for a mouth, taking himself and everything he said to be important, now seemed so comical that the urge to giggle came back in full force. My hand pressed hard over my twitching mouth. Janet looked at the big accusing man and was overwhelmed once more with uncontrollable laughter. It was as if she were enjoying a comedy show.

'Sister Janet, please leave this building now,' the deep earnest voice requested. Then something bordering on revolution took place. Donald stood up in his dreary mac and declared in his dreary voice, 'If Jean goes, I go.'

I hated his audacity, publicly changing Janet's name to Jean. In the stunned silence everybody waited to see what would happen next. Now that I had myself under some control, I removed my hand from my face and formed an expression of shock and disbelief as Donald made his stand against Christianity. But Mr Hulzt seemed lost for words and could only gaze steadfastly at Brother Donald.

'Come on, Jean,' said Donald, taking her arm and shuffling her past the empty benches. Her hysteria had faded and she now looked a bit worried as her ginger-haired champion escorted her out of the church. With the renegades gone, Mr Hulzt continued his gloomy sermon. I felt lonely sitting on the back row on my own, wondering how much chocolate Janet would be given and if I'd ever get a lift home again.

When the grand finale of prayers was over, Aunty Lena rushed up to me and asked what had come over Janet to cause her to behave in such an insulting manner. I couldn't possibly say it was a snot on Brother George's nose, so I said it must have been the Devil.

'Ma poor husband was in agony. To preach the word of God while somebody laughs.' I'd obviously got off scot-free. 'To laugh at the word of God.' Her voice was reaching a crescendo which caused a few of the doddery old Friends to circle us like geriatric sharks, not sure whether they should attack or smile.

'I shall pray for my sister,' I said in my Sunday-best voice, 'that she may realise her sin and ask the Lord for forgiveness.' I had learnt to speak in a stilted, pious manner when the occasion suited. It was amazing that these people couldn't see through me, or maybe they just didn't want to.

'You're a marvel, Deirdre, a tool in the hands of the Lord,' said Aunty Lena. The others nodded approvingly. I was about to say something about the separating of goats and sheep, Janet naturally being a goat, but I thought better of it. Sometimes a hand can be overplayed. The following Sunday, Janet went back to the church and apologised. It was like the return of the prodigal daughter. A great fuss was made of her by everybody and I was practically ignored. I suppose the act of forgiving scores high in heaven and they were all intent on cashing in on it. In his slow, Yorkshire accent Roy Garston asked Janet if she would like a Saturday job working in his fruit shop. 'A nice little job, Janet, three shillings an hour.' He didn't bother asking me if I might like it. Not that I would.

Janet accepted the job, but it only lasted two weeks. She said Roy was always leering at her when she bent over, and staring at her budding breasts. Besides, it was too much like hard work, lugging sacks of spuds and onions about. I reported Brother Roy's behaviour to Aunty Lena, but all she could say was, 'Oh my, how dreadful!'

Things went back to normal with the chocolate, the lifts home in Donald's car and the weariness of hypocrisy. I'd managed to be credited with some award for Bible study while living a double life. I was Deirdre the Devout and Deirdre the Derider (ironically, an anagram of my name). Whatever people required me to be, I would become it. I seemed to be taking on the qualities of the chameleon, changing my opinions, my facial expression and even my voice to suit the company.

But there was something happening in Liverpool at that time, something that took our attention away from the church, from Donald and even from his chocolate. Liverpudlian pop groups were starting to be noticed all over the country, and one of those groups was called the Beatles.

11

The Beatles

I'd never really been in love before until I discovered Paul McCartney. I thought he had beautiful eyes. Beatles pictures were plastered all over the bedroom walls and every Sunday we listened to the top ten on the radio. I thought 'Love Me Do' was the ultimate until I heard 'Please Please Me'.

Janet claimed John Lennon as her own, which left Ringo and George as leftovers. Our obsession had a maternal element to it. It was as if we were adopting a little boy each, rather than dreaming of a romantic liaison with a man. Cushla had a crush on Cliff Richard. For some reason I detested Cliff and a rule was set (in writing) banning any Cliff Richard songs. If 'Summer Holiday' was heard playing on the radio, it was immediately turned off. Cushla went mad at me for violating her rights, but I was bigger than she was, and there was now no father to complain to.

At school I became famous for my McCartney fits. I'd pretend to take an epileptic fit if anything to do with Paul was mentioned. Girls would seek me out at breaktimes to watch the performance and soon Bottom's McCartney Fit was known throughout the school. The fit consisted of violently shaking my head from side to side, waving my hands up and down and screaming 'Paul!' Sometimes, for a special effect, I slobbered saliva down my chin too. This became known as Bottom's Super McCartney Fit, and once this version became established, the previous common or garden seizure was no longer requested. It was physically exhausting performing fits while everybody else sat drinking their little bottles of free milk and being entertained.

Miss Davies, the headmistress, was a small Welsh woman with a terrible temper. One day she called me into her office. She said I was not to perform any more fits in the school grounds as not only was it degrading, but Erica Tomlinson's mother had complained because Erica was a real epileptic and she found my display offensive. It was a relief to hear this. Although I'd become popular, almost a celebrity at school, I was getting headaches every day with shaking my head. The next time somebody sidled up to me in the playground and said the magic words, 'Paul McCartney', I explained how Miss Davies had threatened to expel me if I performed any more fits.

'But if you really loved him, you couldn't help it,' the girl insisted. So to prove that I really loved Paul (nobody else seemed to have to prove their love), the Stifled McCartney Fit evolved. It involved a rigidity of the arms, the head just slightly quivering to one side and the mouth tightly closed, internalising the developing scream which could only be detected as a strangled 'mmmmmm'. This version was much easier on me physically, and after the initial bout of attention, people began to lose interest.

Aunty Lena lived in Allerton, which was where Paul used to live. One day Janet and I decided to visit the Hulzts' home in Wheatcroft Road and have a snoop around the area for the McCartney house in Forthlin Road. It took three different buses to get from Bootle to Allerton, travelling through Penny Lane, which was later to become a famous song.

We felt a little intimidated when we arrived at Aunty Lena's detached house. It had a front garden, a huge back garden and a big garage for the car. We were greeted by the familiar high-pitched voice. 'Come in, lovies, ma husband and I have been so looking forward to seeing you.'

We'd never seen Aunty Lena without her hat on. She looked like someone from the previous century, with her grey hair rolled up around the back of her neck. She wore a short-sleeved dress (home-made of course, lovey) and the tops of her arms were like lumps of jelly hanging from the bones, wobbling about as she moved. I dared not look at Janet for fear of the dreaded giggling. The house had thick carpet in all the rooms, and smelt of freshly baked scones with a hint of disinfectant. Mr Hulzt was sitting in an armchair reading the Bible. On his feet were large, woolly, green slippers with a hand-knitted look about them.

'Good afternoon, young ladies,' he groaned without standing up. He really was like Lurch, the butler from a TV programme we watched called *The Adams Family* – the one who said 'You rang?' in a deep voice. It was going to be agony getting through the visit as already everything began to seem hysterically funny to me, and I knew Janet would be in a similar state, especially on learning that we were to sit at a table and have a proper meal with them. 'Lunch' they called it.

Aunty Lena showed us all the things she had made. All the embroidered cushions, the curtains, the tablecloths, the lace doilies, knitted rugs, woolly slippers, even her handkerchiefs were home-made. When we were left alone for a precious moment, Janet mimicked Aunty Lena's voice: 'I also knitted maself a husband. See what a fine double-gussetted crotch he has, lovey.'

That set off the nervous giggling, but we forced ourselves to look normal when Aunty Lena reappeared with a bowl of salad vegetables. She told us her husband had grown them, as well as many other things, in his vegetable patch which we 'simply must look at' before going home.

We sat at the table with the intimidating figure of Mr Hulzt opposite us. Aunty Lena fussed about with plates and cutlery. I don't think he'd ever really forgiven Janet for her giggling episode at the church. He might have said all the right words but I could tell he bore a grudge. He didn't speak, he just sat with his eyes closed and one big hand on the table, tapping away with his fingers as if he were keeping beat to a song inside his head – probably a hymn. The inside of my cheek hurt as I bit the flesh with my back teeth. From the corner of my eye I could see Janet looking at me, but to turn towards her would be devastating.

All sorts of strange green leaves, sprinkled with chopped-up grass, were dished onto our plates in a no-nonsense manner. Then some delicious smelling, freshly made bread was placed in the middle of the table. Aunty Lena proceeded to dollop a spoonful of mushed-up salmon onto each of our plates. When all the domestic activity had ceased and Aunty Lena was sitting quietly in her chair, Mr Hulzt slowly opened his eyes and had a sly glance about the table before dropping his head forward to pray. The grace wasn't a simple 'For what we are about to receive'. It was detailed and lengthy, a sermon in its own right. It covered the wickedness of this sinful world, the terror of the Last Days, the rising of the dead to be with Christ, the rewards of heaven – 'all for Your glory alone dear Father'.

While they both had their eyes closed, Janet and I pulled faces at the disgusting heap of herbage we were expected to eat. A tiny green-fly was crawling across a leaf on Janet's plate, which caused her to poke about in the salad to see what else there was. This alone was enough to set me off laughing, my eyes hot with tears and my shoulders shaking. I bit my cheek again until the pain was unbearable. The sound of amens signalled the end was nigh. Closing my eyes and emulating an expression of gratitude, I slowly uttered an extra, very reverent amen.

The awful time had come for us to tackle the food. Mr Hulzt closed his eyes while he chewed. He chewed each mouthful about twenty times while his hand lay on the table, his fork tapping away lightly. He said that God made teeth in our mouths, not in our stomachs. When the tapping stopped, he swallowed the food and opened his eyes. He then piled another forkful into his mouth and the tapping started again.

Aunty Lena fussed about piling more salad onto our plates even though we hadn't yet managed the first lot. I felt like dry-retching as my oesophagus revolted at the alien texture of the bland leaves. Janet was having difficulty keeping the food on her fork as it seemed to fall off every time she placed it near her mouth. This gave the appearance of eating without actually swallowing anything. When Aunty Lena disappeared into the kitchen, we quietly scraped all our leaves and grass back into the salad bowl. Mr Hulzt was busy tapping the table, still counting his chews per mouthful.

With knives and forks neatly placed together on the empty plates, we quickly carried them into the kitchen and praised Aunty Lena for 'such a delightful lunch'.

'That's wonderful, lovies,' she beamed, seeing the proof of our praise in the empty plates. After eating a steaming-hot rhubarb pie and custard, we were taken into the back garden to admire the flowers and vegetables. It was tedious work pretending to be interested in runner beans and tomatoes. I asked if I could go to the toilet, not only to escape the dreary lecture on growing vegetables, but also to have a good look at the house.

I noticed they didn't sleep together. There were two single beds in separate rooms. I opened a drawer which contained white linen underwear. Pulling out a pair of underpants I held them up to to the light for a good look. It was hard to say whether they belonged to him or her. They were incredibly long and baggy. I examined them for any trace of skidmarks, but all was pristine white and pure.

Everything had the impression of being hand-made. The toilet paper was in a little linen holder like a tea cosy. It had 'Trust in God' embroidered on it in red-and-blue cotton. It was difficult to imagine either of them doing anything in a toilet – they just didn't seem that type. A small Bible was placed on the cistern. Bibles were all over the house, they were in every room except the bathroom. Downstairs in the front parlour there was an electronic organ and a large blue velvet settee. A bay window had curtains in the same blue velvet. I wondered if Aunty Lena had made the settee too. A bookcase full of black, hard-backed, boring looking books stood in the corner. At first I thought they were all Bibles, but they might as well have been. They were all on Christianity.

'Are you all right, lovey?' called out Aunty Lena at the bottom of the stairs. I emerged from the parlour saying I'd managed to get a bit lost in their beautiful big home. It was easy to make Aunty Lena beam with delight. She laughed her horsey laugh and directed me back outside towards the vegetables.

They didn't seem to have any sort of a pet, not even a budgie or a goldfish. The garden would have been ideal for a dog and there was a big wooded park directly behind them. When I asked Aunty Lena if they owned any pets she snorted a laugh, saying, 'Oh my, lovey!' as if some totally ridiculous question had been asked.

At last the time came for us to leave. Laden down with bunches of spinach and bags of beans, we decided to search for Forthlin Road where Paul McCartney lived. As we didn't have a map and the whole area of Allerton, as far as the eye could see, was made up of detached and semi-detached houses with gardens and no doubt bathrooms, I concluded that Paul must come from a posh background. It was disappointing to find this out. Although he was called a lad from Liverpool, it wasn't from an area like Bootle. There was no getting away from it: Paul McCartney was posh.

On the bus rides home Janet and I discussed our visit to the Hulzts. I told her about the immaculate underpants and the dozens of Bibles placed all over the house. She said she'd been subjected to torture by lecture – on the best times to plant seeds and how often things should be watered. We wondered who the Hulzts would leave all their money to when they died. They didn't have any children and they didn't like pets. We wondered if we might inherit something. But our wondering in that direction didn't last long. We realised simultaneously with a flash of insight where their fortune would end up – setting up a home for unwanted Bibles!

My mum looked at the spinach and runner beans with a disapproving, upturned lip. We only ever had cabbage, Brussels sprouts or soggy peas at home. As she didn't know what to do with them, and we explained how they were tasteless leaves and stalks that only posh people ate, they ended up in the bin. That night we had fish and chips for tea (to compensate for the unpalatable lunch) with plenty of salt and vinegar and soggy peas. Delicious.

Everybody at school was talking about the Beatles concert, which was to be held at the Liverpool Empire. My mum gave

Janet and me the money for tickets. I don't know how she managed to put money away, but she did. This concert was an emotional emergency, something the savings had to be spent on. She seemed to understand how we felt; after all, she'd been in love with Mario Lanza, and if he had ever come to Liverpool, somehow she would have managed to see him.

I began wearing a black polo-neck sweater under my school uniform. The polo-neck was squashed down so it didn't show, but I made sure the other girls knew I was breaking the school rules. It was a token of loyalty to the Beatles. Other girls began to copy me.

There was a large, dark-haired teacher called Mrs Jones. She was Welsh, and like Miss Davies she had a ferocious temper. A dark moustache glistened over her top lip. Being fat, the size of her thighs caused her to sit at her desk with her legs open. Her desk was at the front of the class, and during the geography lesson Valerie and I pretended to drop our pens so we could bend down and peep up her skirt. We called her Jellylegs, that being the sight we encountered. From where her stockings ended and her baggy knickers began, there were two lumps of grey-white jelly.

One day I was caught. I'd become careless, and stooping down I looked back at Valerie as I giggled at the sight. 'Deirdre Rammsbottom!' Mrs Jones called out. The sound of the name jolted me like an electric shock. It created a murmur of sniggering in the class, and I was led away in shame to Miss Davies' room to await punishment.

'What exactly were you looking for?' Miss Davies' little Aryan blue eyes glared at me throughout the interrogation. I wanted to shock her by telling the truth, to see her reaction. But in the circumstances I decided a lie might be better. Both the Welsh teachers were standing over me, itching to start the punishing. I hated Miss Davies' tight, curly, white-blond hair, cut severely short with a quiff of frizzy, angry curls in the front. 'I dropped me pen and was in the middle of picking it up....'

'Don't lie to me!' Miss Davies' lower jaw was jutting out, making her look like some breed of Albino baboon. 'Now the truth please, my girl.'

Looking her straight in the eye I remained defiantly silent. I decided to be like Christ before Pilate and say nothing. Unfortunately a small piece of black polo-neck sweater was sticking out over my collar. There was further interrogation. I was made to undo my blouse and gymslip and take the sweater off in front of them. It was thrown with contempt into the bin. I was now a martyr in the hands of Barbarians.

'Do you know what this is?' asked Miss Davies, lifting a long bamboo cane from a shelf. 'I said do you know what this is, Miss Rammsbottom? Are you deaf as well as daft?'

A feeling of hot anger was spreading over me like a prickly rash. The teachers seemed to know that my name itself was the biggest insult they could throw at me. The cane quivered in anticipation under my nose. 'Of course I know what it is,' I shouted. 'It's a cane for hittin' girls with.'

Miss Davies' mouth became more ape-like than ever and her curly quiff of hair seemed to stand on end with rage. 'Don't you ever "of course" me while you're at this school!'

Mrs Jones was now looking a bit concerned. She had caused it, sitting in front of a class of bored, restless young girls with her hairy legs open, inviting inspection, while droning on about latitude and longitude. What else were we supposed to do?

'Take hold of her hand,' the headmistress ordered Mrs Jones. My left hand was placed out, palm facing up. I could see a flicker of sadistic joy in Miss Davies' face as she raised the cane. It made a whirring sound as it came down hard upon my flesh. The pain was excruciating and I started to cry. But I wasn't to be let off with only one whack. Miss Davies raised her right arm further back for good impact, causing her left leg to rise up off the ground. Then arm, cane and leg came down together for the second whack. Mrs Jones still held my hand out and I could tell she was starting to feel sorry for me. The angry strength in her grip had gone and I pulled my burning hand to my breast and cradled it.

'It's three you're getting,' said Miss Davies, quickly raising the cane again. But I wasn't going to let her hurt my poor hand anymore. As Mrs Jones tried to get hold of me, I turned towards the door and ran out. I ran out of the school and down Balliol Road to the Education Board offices to report a case of theft and violence. A middle-aged woman wearing horn-rimmed glasses told me to go back to school and to stop wasting their precious time. But the pain in my hand made me bold and I refused. I sat in the reception area and asked to see the manager. Eventually a young man came out and I showed him my red stinging hand. I explained how I'd been attacked with a stick by two mad Welsh teachers, and that they'd also stolen my jumper. He asked me for the names of the teachers and wrote something on a sheet of paper. Then he asked me what my name was, but I couldn't say it.

'You can't file a complaint without saying who you are,' he said. He had lovely green-coloured eyes emanating sympathy and kindness. I wondered what his name was.

'Me name's Deirdre, and that's all I wanna put,' I said. The young man went away for a while and came back.

'I've phoned the school and everything's been sorted out, so you can go back now. Nothing will happen to you.'

'What about me Beatles jumper?' I asked. He assured me that I would get it back, but I mustn't wear it for school, not even

A Dandelion By Any Other Name

under my uniform. After thanking him for his help, I asked what his name was. It was John Tindell. Walking back to school I sounded out the name, Deirdre Tindell, and imagined three children, two boys and a girl, all with large green eyes. Paul, John and Lynnette Tindell. All of us living happily ever after in a semi-detached in Allerton.

I'd only been back at school for an hour when I was arrested by two monitors and brought to the headmistress's office. There I was given the promised third whack of the cane by the woman who would have been quite at home in the Gestapo. I didn't get my black polo-neck jumper back, either. I don't know who John Tindell had been speaking to on the phone, if he'd been phoning at all. I preferred to believe he'd contacted the wrong school, which just happened to have a Miss Davies and a Mrs Jones, who had just that morning caned a girl called Deirdre. A different Deirdre.

The great day arrived when the Beatles were to perform at the Liverpool Empire. The place was full of teenaged girls in a high state of excitement. Janet and I had taken care to look as attractive as we could. Wearing lipstick and black eye-liner, I practised my Jane Asher smile in the mirror. Janet didn't seem to suit wearing make-up. I told her she looked like a clown and that John probably wouldn't fancy her. She told me I looked like a tart.

It was disappointing to find ourselves seated right near the back looking down onto a tiny stage. Some other group came on first and almost everybody in the audience fidgeted and chatted all the way through their performance. At last the curtain went up for the Beatles. From where we sat we couldn't even distinguish who was who (apart from Ringo on the drums). Three miniature figures moved about on the stage. The audience went into a frenzy. Everybody stood up and waved their arms, screaming for their particular idol to take notice of them. Every girl was screaming one of the four names at the stage. There was no hope of hearing the music.

I worked out which tiny figure was Paul. He had the left-handed guitar. For some reason we didn't bother screaming or waving. Instead Janet and I spent much of the time crouching about on the floor. Somebody had spilt a whole box of Cadbury's Roses, but with the wild commotion going on it hadn't been noticed, except of course by us. On our hands and knees, hidden by a sea of hysterical girls, we quickly collected all the chocolates and hid them in our pockets. Then we stood up, joining the noisy audience and slyly sneaked one chocolate after another into our mouths, letting the colourful empty wrappers flutter to the floor.

A girl next to me (probably the owner of the chocolates) was going berserk. Tears rolled down her cheeks as she held her outstretched arms towards the stage calling for George. Sucking on a strawberry cream I calmly observed her. She looked really stupid. There were hundreds of girls doing the same sort of thing. I thought about my McCartney fit. If I threw one here, nobody would notice, least of all Paul. Sliding my hand into my pocket, I unwrapped another chocolate.

In the cold air of Lime Street Janet and I waited for a bus back to Bootle. The noise throughout the concert had been deafening. We weren't sure what songs the Beatles had sung, although a few 'yeah yeah yeahs' of 'She Loves You' had been audible. I wondered what the Beatles themselves had thought of the audience. Were they annoyed? A whole audience of supposedly devoted fans not listening to a note of their music.

Upstairs in our bedroom, with the walls full of Beatles pictures, I felt closer to Paul, John, George and Ringo than I had seeing them in real life. Janet counted how many Roses chocolates we

A Dandelion By Any Other Name

had left: only six. We lay on the bed looking at the pictures while quietly finishing them off. My favourite picture was of the Beatles wearing old-fashioned swimming costumes. I stared at Paul's hairy legs and wondered about my life. Who would I end up marrying? Probably not Paul McCartney. Definitely not Cliff Richard. Some lad from Canal Street called Joey McScinty had been looking at me with intent lately. It was a pity about the name. Still, it wasn't in the same league as my current one. 'McScinty' would be fine by me.

12

The Snogging Grounds

It was a time when the old port of Liverpool became more associated with the Beatles and pop music than with its own maritime history. Other Merseyside groups such as Gerry and the Pacemakers, The Merseybeats and The Searchers were also climbing the British musical charts. As Liverpudlian penpals had now become very much sought after, especially by American teenagers, I decided to join an international penpal club at school. I began writing to a girl from Los Angeles called Dixie. I wrote and nonchalantly explained how we practically lived next door to Paul, and how we didn't make much fuss of them over here. After all, they were just a few lads from Liverpool who could sing. I signed my name Deirdre Roberts.

It must have caused quite a stir, because within a few weeks dozens of requests from American girls for Beatle autographs were arriving at our house. Good American greenbacks were offered and their orders were diligently filled. I practised very hard forging the Beatles' signatures, and it was George Harrison's that I managed to perfect. Consequently lots of George Harrison autographs were flown across the Atlantic Ocean and lots of American dollars came back. The American currency was exchanged at a variety of banks for British pounds. It was spent on make-up, clothes and, of course, chocolates.

'What sort of business is goin' on here then?' The postman was becoming suspicious. Every day bulky letters were arriving from America. My mum warned me I'd end up in Walton Gaol on fraud charges. It was a lucrative little enterprise but the postman's suspicious comments frightened me. I stopped replying to the letters and gradually they stopped coming.

Resolving to go straight, I began to concentrate on my main goal in life in eanest. Armed with make-up and new clothes from my forgeries, I was like a tiger on the prowl – the prey being a husband. I was fifteen years old and about to leave school. All I wanted was a new name to enable me to start living a proper life.

I applied for an office job in an insurance company. Janet taunted me with how things would be there. She said the boss would slowly begin to fancy me. Then one day he would come up close, remove my horn-rimmed glasses (the fact that I didn't wear glasses made no impact on her predictions), then he would gently untie the back of my hair, letting the long tresses fall about my shoulders, then say with a pleasant surprise – 'but . . . why, Miss Rammsbottom!'

I got the job and on the following Friday I left school forever. That Friday, I experienced great joy in throwing muddy clods of grass all over the headmistress's white car. Janet told me there was a full assembly on the Monday morning to try and find out 'what sort of hooligan' was responsible.

In my new job I had to locate files from thousands of brown cardboard folders that were stacked in area order – Bradford, Chester, Derby, etc – and then client name order. I worked with a small, extremely thin man called Mr Blackburn, who was supposed to have been starved and beaten as a Japanese prisoner of war. Because of his stature, I helped him locate Sheffied, Stoke and Scunthorpe files which were kept on the top shelf. I didn't mind doing this for him as he never tried to peer up my skirt when I climbed the ladder. I think the Japanese harmed him in many different ways.

It was a great relief to find that people at work addressed me as Deirdre and not Miss Rammsbottom. My direct supervisor was a pleasant, middle-aged woman called May. There were lots of middle-aged spinsters in the company. Most of them had fiancés or boyfriends who were killed during the war, and out of loyalty or lack of opportunity they had remained single.

Apart from Mr Blackburn, there seemed to be only two other males in the whole company. One was the manager, Mr Jacobson, an older man with drooping jowls like a spaniel; the other was a storeman called Bob, who was short, bald and married. From that selection I couldn't see Janet's prediction coming true. It was about a week later I discovered there were other males who worked downstairs, underground in the archives department. Very old files were kept down there and one afternoon I was sent down to find a long-lost client, John Smith from Bolton.

Two young men wearing grubby calico workcoats were sitting in the gloomy light on wooden stools. The clacking of my heels on the stone staircase caused them to turn round and look at me. One of them was spotty with a front tooth missing. The other was a bit squinty-eyed and looked as though he'd spent more than his working life in this subterranean world of insurance archives. In the dim light they resembled wax dummies discarded from Madame Tussauds – rejects from the Chamber of Horrors. But they were the right sex and, for me, a serendipitous find.

I pretended to be more helpless and dim-witted than I really was, so they could feel superior. Then, as with most young males, they started to show off. They were like birds, flapping their wings to impress the dull brown peahen. I wondered what their names were. Later on that day I found out they were Eddie Thorn and Terry Martindale. From the two I thought Martindale would be the better name, but there was nothing wrong with 'Thorn'.

Each day I grabbed all the Smiths and Jones clients in the hope of having to venture downstairs for old files. But this small glimmer of hope didn't last long. The two troglodytes were sacked. Nobody was sure what they'd done or hadn't done to deserve being fired. They were replaced by one middle-aged woman working part-time hours.

As my prospects for securing a husband at work weren't looking so great, I decided to concentrate on Joey McScinty from Canal Street, at least until something better turned up. By now I had my own genuine pair of small breasts which I promoted as best I could without looking too much like a sergeant major. One Saturday afternoon I stood at the gate and waited for Joey to walk past. Pat Gawler was on lookout duty for her mother. She poked her tongue out at me, her eyes squinting in the sun. I stood my ground, not allowing her obnoxious grimaces or staring to intimidate me. Eventually Joey McScinty and his mate Peter Adams walked past as they usually did about that time.

'Iyer,' I said, catching Joey's eye. Desperation for a marriage partner had made me plucky.

'Iyer,' he answered back, looking at Peter for some support and then back at me. Both lads stopped outside our gate, their hands remaining rigid inside their jacket pockets while they shifted awkwardly from foot to foot, as if cold. Watching the situation closely, Pat Gawler was on full alert, her hands on her big hips, ready for anything.

'What are yer doin' tonight?' Joey asked me staring at my

breasts, which were poking out like missiles thanks to a new pointy bra.

'Nothink,' I answered, eyeing his mate Peter.

There was some more shuffling about as Joey mustered up courage. 'Wanna have a snog then?' he finally asked.

I didn't want to appear too eager, so I gazed down at the ground and bit my lower lip as though concentrating on making a tough decision. 'Okay,' I answered. 'I'll see yer about seven then.' His head nodded towards the debris, the snogging ground for young lovers, and the not so young. I agreed. As the two lads walked away, they both spat simultaneously at the ground. They were trying to impress me with their spitting prowess. I was the female and I had choices, but I didn't examine the gobs of spit to see who was the better prospect. I ran inside and put my hair in curlers ready for my first date.

'Where yer goin'?' Janet asked, sensing something special might be happening. I told her I was going out on a date with Joey McScinty from Canal Street. 'Him? He always has snot runnin' out his nose,' she assured me. I told her she was just jealous because all she could get was dirty old Donald. My mum said Joey's surname was worse than ours – an opinion truly worthy of contempt.

The afternoon was spent ironing my best dress, giving myself a good all-over wash in the sink and making up my face in the mirror. After taking the curlers out and brushing my hair, I thought I looked quite attractive. Certainly attractive enough to hook myself some sort of a mate.

That evening I met Joey at seven o'clock. He'd secured a little corner of the debris for us, right next to the back-entry where the bins were. It was almost dark so we got straight down to business. He put his hand on my right breast and pressed his open mouth against mine. His teeth were prominent and I could feel his tongue, like an eel slithering about in my mouth. A dribble of his saliva oozed down my chin. It was not a pleasant experience. In fact I felt on the verge of vomiting. The thought of either putting up with this romantic style for the rest of my life or being left with my dreadful name was frightening. Pulling my head away to breathe I suggested we might like to talk instead.

'What d'yer wanna talk for?' he asked, as I unscrewed his hand from my mauled right breast. I asked him if he liked me. 'Can't yer tell?' he said, returning his grip.

'Maybe we should go for a walk,' I suggested. 'Along Stanley Road to look in the furniture shops.'

'What's wrong with here?' he asked, obviously feeling put out. He had small green eyes and straight brown hair. I imagined the children, dribbling mouths and snotty noses. But I would be a McScinty and so would they.

Without warning he pounced, and began again the mouth-to-mouth resuscitation. This time his other hand began to work its way up my thigh towards my bum. I was pinned by two hands and a mouth, and something stiffening further down with a power all of its own. My head and body were pressed hard against the concrete wall, with hands kneading at my breast and buttock as if I was dough. His teeth gnawed at my mouth. I managed a muffled scream as I struggled, but this was interpreted as passion, and he pressed his whole gangly body even harder against mine.

Suddenly there was a light shining and giggly girlish laughter coming from behind us. Joey let go of me and turned around to see who it was. Janet and Cushla were perched up on our backyard wall with a torch. Out of his grip, I bolted towards our front gate. Joey ran after me but I managed to close the gate between us. I told him I was going inside to sort out my sisters.

He tried to offer me the comforts and privacy of the back-entry instead, but I'd experienced enough.

'I've got a headache,' I said, putting my hand against my head. 'I'll see yer around.' Banging the door shut, I rushed to the kitchen sink and washed my face with a flannel and soap. Janet and Cushla came in and asked what it had been like.

'We saw yer gettin' felt,' said Cushla, beaming with mischief. I told them he was my boyfriend and that he was in love with me. That he might want to marry me. I never told them that his probing tongue and rough hands had made me feel sick. But I'd have to get used to that sort of thing. And to have children, I knew I'd have to let him do far worse things. A few days later I developed a lower lip full of cold sores, a painful reminder of my Don Juan from Canal Street.

For some reason, the following Saturday night Joey didn't turn up for our second date. I had decided to tell him I couldn't kiss because of my traumatised mouth, and instead we could look at rings in the jewellery shop in Strand Road. I heard later he was 'going with' Pat Gawler instead, and that I was a stuck-up bitch, but Pat was a 'real goer'. I couldn't believe it.

'There's more fish in the sea,' my mum informed me.

'God, that's original, isn't it?' I snarled, picking the last bit of crusty scab from my lower lip.

They say God moves in mysterious ways. One Monday evening, while we were watching *The Saint*, there was a weak, hesitant knocking at the door. It was a young vicar from some church near Trinity Road. My mum brought him into our living room as he wanted to speak to the young ladies or gentlemen of the house. On hearing this, I turned the TV volume down, but Cushla fancied Roger Moore and turned it back up again. The vicar, sensing a row was about to start, suggested we use another room. Janet and I, flattered at being called young ladies, quickly ushered him into the front parlour.

He told us there was a new youth club opening in Trinity Road the following Friday night and hoped we could come along.

'What d'yer have to do there?' I asked, worried I might have to play table tennis or worse.

'You just come along and associate with other young people in a Christian atmosphere,' he answered. We agreed to give it a go, even though the idea of a 'Christian atmosphere' was a bit off-putting. He was quite nice looking for a vicar. I noticed he was wearing a wedding ring.

'I suppose I should check with your mother,' he said. 'After all, it doesn't finish until ten o'clock.' We assured him our mother wouldn't mind us going. Taking a notebook from his pocket, he asked us our names. The familiar feeling of shame crept over me. I was sick of having to tell lies.

'And you are?' he was looking at Janet. She could lead this time and I would follow. She normally chose the name Randell. My insides twisted with alarm as Janet stated her full true name – Janet Rammsbottom. The vicar gave a little laugh and continued looking at Janet, his pen still poised. He thought she was having him on. But when he saw my embarrassed, reddening face he wrote the name in his book. I said I was Janet's sister, Deirdre.

When the vicar left, and after I'd rebuked Janet for being honest, a great sense of hope and excitement welled up inside me, swamping the usual fear. I imagined the youth club swarming with nice-looking young men, all desperate to get married. It was a shame they might be dim-witted Christians, but I could live with that.

It was unbelievable how stubborn and unreasonable Janet had

become. At half-past six on the Friday evening she said she couldn't be bothered going to the youth club. She preferred to watch *Bonanza* on TV. She was now in love with Adam Cartwright and said she would rather have him than a spotty Christian. My friend Valerie had a bad cold and couldn't come either. I had to go on my own.

Wearing a pink, tightly fitting coat (which nicely emphasised my figure), I walked through the dark streets to the new youth club. It was a crispy cold night as I flounced along Trinity Road, and the click-clack-click of my high heels on the stone pavement echoed in the silence, stating my presence – a female on the prowl.

The club was inside a brightly lit church hall. Standing outside I could hear voices, male voices talking and laughing. Although nervous, I knew therein lay my salvation. All I had to do was to put one foot in front of the other until I was inside the club. I ordered my body to start walking. The vicar greeted me, and even remembered my name, introducing me as Deirdre to three young men. They gazed at me and I could tell they thought I was attractive. They nudged each other and made silly yokel-type sounds. But the attention only lasted a few minutes. Being Christians, they soon continued fiddling about with pieces of wood, as though I wasn't there.

They were the sort of people who laugh at anything. I tried to join in on the fun, but it was difficult. Their humour mainly consisted of goonish sounds and repeating the words nick-nack-nicky-nacky-noo in a sing-song fashion. One of them kept asking me, with a deadly serious expression, if I knew I had a kneecap half way down my leg. They thought they were fantastic wits. One of them was called Tony. He had a sparse beard, which barely covered a face full of pimples, and wore scruffy leather sandals.

This was unusual, as most Christians tended to be squeaky clean. I decided he must be a keen Jesus fan, until I found out later he was a university student. That seemed to explain everything.

The other two were John, big-nosed, gangly with tight curly hair, and Mike, shorter, freckly with sticky-out ears. They both had that special wholesome Christian look about them. After five minutes of listening to their high-pitched yahooing humour and being ignored, I decided to leave. Just as I was moving towards the door, three more people arrived. Two males and a female. They looked quite normal compared to the wood-fiddlers, so I sat down again and watched.

One of the young men was called James. He had beautiful eyes with long eyelashes and fair wavy hair. He sat next to me, initiating conversation. We talked easily. He only had a slight Liverpudlian accent because he'd spent much of his life in Wales. I tried to impress him with some lines I knew from *Macbeth* and *Hamlet*, but he didn't seem to pick up on them. I assumed that people from Wales would be interested in Shakespeare, especially with all those old Welsh castles scattered about.

Soon it was ten o'clock and the club was closing. James walked me all the way home. When my mum appeared at our front door, he quickly said goodnight. 'I'll see yer at the club next Friday then,' I said. He didn't even try to kiss or touch me, probably thinking my mum might be the type of mother who would disapprove.

I watched him walk jauntily across the road and disappear into the darkness. My knees were weak with hope. 'Who's that?' my mum asked.

'Some feller'.

He certainly was some feller. All week I thought about him and imagined all sorts of wondrous domestic happenings for the near future. I'd been so enthralled by James, I'd forgotten to find out what his surname was. It could be Winterbottom for all I knew. Thank God he hadn't inquired after mine, because I really didn't want to deceive him. Not if he was going to be my future husband, the father of my children.

The following Friday, the three bores and the vicar were in the club when I arrived. I said hello, then sat down to watch the door. James arrived on his own. He came straight towards me and smiled. 'Had a good week?' he asked, settling himself on a stool next to me.

'Yeh, I suppose it was all right.' It was important to appear nonchalant, like part of a game I had to play. Softly, softly catches monkey.

He bought two lemonades from the club bar and we sat talking. Once again the conversation came easily. This time I remembered to ask the all-important question. With a great warm pleasure I took in the answer. James Mortimer. Mortimer! A wonderful name that conjured up nothing.

He seemed to be interested in country life as he often talked about his childhood in Wales. I told him I was really a country girl at heart, that I loved gardening. I thanked God Janet wasn't there to hear. My only experience with gardening was digging up a couple of dead cats we'd once buried, to see how far the disintegration process had progressed. 'Yeah, I love gardenin', yer know, growin' vegetables and all that.'

As James walked me home I asked him if he was a Christian, and he said he probably was. When I tried to debate some points regarding Christian beliefs, he just shrugged and said he didn't really take much interest in it all. He had such lovely eyes, I couldn't stop looking at him. I envied his long eyelashes and decided I would have them anyway, along with his name, for my children.

When we reached our house in Berry Street I was horrified to see Mrs Gawler on late shift at her gate. Her body stiffened with interest when she saw us and she stared aggressively in our direction. 'Take no notice' I whispered to James. 'She's just a nosy neighbour.' Suddenly, he leaned his head towards me and gave me a kiss. His lips were soft and sensual. Straightening up, he knocked on the door. When my mum appeared, he waved goodbye, saying he'd see me next Friday at the club. I stood full of emotion, watching as he walked away.

'Who the fuck's he then?' asked Mrs Gawler. It was nice to have such concerned neighbours.

'None of your business,' I answered, closing the door with a bang as I went inside. I decided that the next time James walked me home, I'd introduce him to my mum, as long as she promised not to embarrass me. She could smile and nod, but she mustn't speak or fart.

At work I talked about my boyfriend to the other women. How we were thinking of getting engaged soon, and maybe going on a holiday to Jersey together. They all seemed quite interested and I enjoyed the status it endowed. Paul McCartney suddenly lost all his magic. James was real and my life now had real prospects.

On Thursday afternoon I pretended to feel sick at work. Instead of going home I went to Blacklers and bought a tiny pair of baby's bootees. They were made of yellow fluffy wool with little bobbles at the front. On the train going home I held them close to my heart. I was almost sixteen years old and already full of maternal longing.

13

'Men Go Mad for Sex'

The following week I left the club in tears. James had not turned up. I'd sat on a hard wooden stool with a glass of flat lemonade for two hours. Obviously feeling sorry for me, the vicar tried his best to keep me company. He told me James just lived around the corner in Beckham Place, number 23. On the way home, I glanced down the small cul-de-sac called Beckham Place. Walking a few yards along I stopped outside number 23. It was an old three-storey house with a large, well-maintained front garden. There was a grey van parked in the drive.

Nobody seemed to acknowledge my knocking on the door so I rang the doorbell. It was the first time in my life I'd ever pressed a doorbell. The synthetically cheerful ding-dong sound soon produced a short plump woman with blonde hair and dark roots. 'Is James there please?' I asked as nicely as possible. She told me her son James had dropped a piece of marble on his foot at work and was lying on the couch if I wanted to see him. A combination of shame and concern left me unable to decide if I wanted to see him or not. The woman was becoming slightly agitated, wanting to close the door on my indecision.

'Could you just tell him Deirdre called?' She said she would.

The night became beautiful. Thousands of stars were glimmering in the clear cold sky. I imagined my dad up there, a spirit dwelling on some special star where dead people go. 'Hello dad,' I whispered towards the sky. The sound of my own breathy voice made me feel a bit silly. But I felt that he, my dad, did continue to live, existing without the need for a body, and was now all-knowing and more kindly than he had been on earth.

The air was fresh and crisp. I began to feel a pleasure in my own breathing. I became conscious of my body, my legs in perfect balance, one foot swinging in front of the other, moving me along in any direction my mind steered it. I became aware of all my senses – sight, sound, smell, singing. Yes, there was a sense of music, too. I felt alive and joyful.

I wondered about evolution. Was I just part of a long slow progression? An animal walking on its hind legs, with all its faculties for survival? Or was I part of something divine with a soul? Tonight I was a soul inhabiting its own breathing body. 'Hello dad,' I whispered again to the sky, but this time I didn't feel silly. It was one soul acknowledging the existence of another.

My elation was soon dampened when ginger-haired Teddy Gawler stopped me as I walked through the subway. He held my arm with a hard, uncompromising grip. 'What are yer frightened of?' he asked, putting his face right up to mine. Like all the Gawlers, there was something porcine about him. His flesh was like pork with spiky hairs growing on it. Because of a turn in his left eye, one eye looked at me while the other looked sideways. He was so aesthetically unappealing, I preferred to look at the grimy, graffiti-covered wall of the subway.

'I know what yer frightened of,' he said. 'It's sexual intercourse, isn't it? You're a virgin.'

I could smell alcohol on his breath, and he could probably

smell fear on mine. He wore a woollen red-and-green V-neck jersey that was far too tight for him and which smelt of stale food. I tried to struggle free but his grip remained firm. My arm and shoulder were hurting and I thought of poking him in the eye (the one looking sideways), but felt repulsed when I imagined my finger slithering through his mushy head.

Male voices could be heard approaching the top of the subway. 'Get off will yer!' I screamed, hoping the approaching men would hear. Two of them immediately started running towards us.

'Are you all right, love?' asked one of them as I tried to shove Teddy away from me.

'No!' I screamed. 'I'm not all right.'

'Mind yer own fuckin' business,' slurred Teddy, his asymmetrical eyes half closing with inebriation.

With one final yank on Teddy's arm, I was free and ran off like a wild creature escaping from a trap. I didn't even stay to say thank you to my rescuers. There was a sound of fists punching into flesh followed by groaning. When I turned round and looked back down the dark subway, I could make out the silhouettes of one person on the ground and two standing over him kicking. Animals I decided. We're all just animals.

That night I set myself a written goal, signing and dating it. My goal was to be married by this time next year. Marriage held many benefits and would solve most of my problems. A new name, the higher societal status bestowed on the married woman, and the safety of a permanent escort. I would prefer the husband to be James, but I was not confident enough to add his name to the goal. Not yet anyway.

James and I decided to quit the youth club. Friday and Saturday nights became our nights out. He took me to a place I'd never been before, a Chinese restaurant. It was called the Golden Phoenix and I ordered Chinese roast pork with fried rice and mushrooms, number 47 on the menu. Every time we ate there, which was almost every Saturday night, I ordered the same meal as it was so delicious. I didn't even want to try anything else. Number 47 with mushroom extra was perfect. We also sat at the same corner table every time. It became our table in our restaurant. The Toys singing 'The Lovers' Concerto' became our song.

James was a marble mason. His creative output consisted mainly of gravestones, but sometimes he made more elaborate things such as marble angels and roses. When we went for a walk through Bootle cemetery he would point out the gravestones he had made himself. Blocks of black-speckled granite and smooth, white, Italian marble. What a strange job it seemed, creating finely polished slabs of stone to mark places in the ground where corpses lie rotting. But James took a great pride in his work and called himself an artist. He showed me how he inconspicuously left his initials at the bottom of the gravestones. It seemed funny that his name should be on dozens of gravestones instead of just the one like everybody else.

After a few weeks of going out together, James invited me back to his parents' house in Beckham Place. On being introduced, his dad stood up when I entered the room, shook my hand and grinned, displaying a mouth full of rotten teeth. Then he went back to his armchair and continued to watch TV. His mother was slightly cooler. She said hello and smiled, but made sure I didn't feel very welcome.

They had things, the Mortimers did. Things that could define people, place them in a higher category. A telephone, a bathroom, an inside toilet, a van and a big garden, not to mention the doorbell. Because of these things, the Mortimers seemed (to me anyway) to be middle class while I (because of my lack of things) belonged more to the working class. At the end of the house there was a little back sitting-room where James and I sat together on an old brown leather couch. After talking for a while, James would turn the light off and our kissing sessions would begin. I liked kissing him. The kissing made our hands restless, wanting to touch each other's bodies. It all seemed to be related.

After three months of seeing each other there was still no sign of a proposal. James bought me boxes of chocolates which I hoarded in the top drawer. I wouldn't open them, but would often bring them out to parade before Cushla and Janet. Boxes of Black Magic and Cadbury's Milk Tray with double layers. I enjoyed watching my sisters' eyes light up, thinking I was going to open them. Foolish virgins.

Receiving chocolates was fine, and being taken to restaurants was a luxury, but it was marriage I was now wanting. It was time for sex. 'Men go mad for sex,' my mum said. She explained how most women just put up with it, but men loved it, thrived on it. They'd do anything for it. Anything.

Janet agreed to stay out of the way on the following Saturday afternoon. I changed the flannelette sheets on our bed and hoovered the floor. James turned up at two o'clock, following me upstairs to the bedroom. I told him I'd like to have some sex please. He seemed quite happy to oblige.

After removing our clothes we lay on the bed kissing. It was obvious James was ready for the next stage. His body frightened me. My own female body frightened me. My two breasts like small pears, the widened hips and the triangle of dark hair all seemed to be part of a very sacred piece of equipment. I had a womb where babies could develop. I could grow other human beings inside me. An exhilarating feeling took over when I observed our natural states. Not just a physical excitement, but the deep emotional thrill of knowing that a child could be created with these two naked bodies.

I opened my legs and James lay on top of me. There was a problem. Being a virgin, James was having difficulty penetrating me. It was like a battering-ram against a closed door, but finally the door gave way and he was inside me. I felt no erotic thrill, only a slight physical stinging. But the magical power of reproduction was seducing. My body writhed under his in some primitive dance of creation. 'D'yer like me?' I asked him, ever the opportunist. He nodded with a contorted face while his hips moved up and down. 'D'yer love me?' I continued, taking full advantage of the situation. In a short volley of grunts, he said he thought he might. It was only a might, but it was better than nothing.

In this position, even though I was underneath a man, I felt a great sense of power. A power derived through sex. I had a female body, and as well as being able to create new people I could acquire what I wanted from men. Make them say things, promise things they may not normally agree to.

Afterwards we lay together cuddling. He said I was good in bed. 'Am I?' I asked, not really sure what he meant but knew it to be a compliment. Soon we both drifted into a peaceful sleep. We were wakened by Cushla shouting downstairs. James was worried about my mum finding us, but I explained she wasn't like his mother. Watching James put his clothes on I felt a sense of propriety. My husband. The father of my children.

Once dressed, we walked downstairs together and made a cup of tea. Cushla was shy of James and when he asked her what her name was, thankfully she didn't answer. I had to tell him some day, but not yet. At least he wouldn't be taking mine for his own. I thanked God I wasn't the male.

A few weeks later, in July I noticed myself in the mirror. My eyes were bright with happiness. My period was three days overdue, and I just knew it had finally happened. The person looking back at me in the mirror was now carrying a child. I decided to wait another two weeks before going to the doctor for confirmation. The yellow bootees were put in a special drawer lined with tissue paper, along with a white lace bib and a little blue hairbrush. Janet knew about my secret collection and she knew I'd become desperate for a baby. I didn't tell anybody else, not even James. One thing I was sure of: there was no way my baby was going to be born with the name Rammsbottom. Once the doctor confirmed the pregnancy, I would tell James and he would have no choice but to marry me.

It was about two o'clock in the morning when it started. Great flashes of lightning followed by the loudest thunder we had ever heard. Janet and I were terrified. Spasmodic flashes of lightning lit up our bedroom in a ghostly brightness and thunder boomed directly overhead, crashing loudly as though something huge was banging on the roof.

Wearing only our summer nighties, we raced along the landing to the next room and climbed into my mum's double bed. Cushla was already there. The four of us huddled together in the big bed, covering our heads with the blankets. My mum said the thunder was louder than the bombs during the war. The lightning was so bright we could still see it underneath the blankets. For hours the storm raged directly overhead. Armageddon was upon us.

Cushla and Janet were crying as my mum assured us in a whispering voice that we'd all be found 'burnt to a crisp' in the morning. Optimism had never been one of her strong points. Every New Year's Eve at the stroke of twelve she would shudder and whisper, 'Oh God, I wonder what the new year's got in store for us?' Other people celebrated Hogmanay by clicking glasses together and singing; my mum only ever shuddered.

Outside, the storm still raged. 'Ooh Jesus help us!' The whispering of the oracle continued under the blankets, 'they'll find four black, charred bodies in the bed, and they'll know it was us.' My heart thumped with fear. I didn't want to be burnt to death. It was the worst, most painful death to endure. And my poor baby, I wanted to see what he'd be like. Would he have brown eyes like me, or blue eyes like his father? I lay rigid, my nose now out from under the blankets waiting for the smell of the burning house, waiting with each flash of lightning for the fire. The thunder itself seemed fierce enough to start a fire, even if the lightning didn't. I put my hands against my womb, protecting my tiny baby. His name was going to be Matthew, meaning 'A gift from God'.

But the predictions of our whispering oracle were wrong. The thunderclaps became fainter, gradually changing to a rumbling in the distance. It was as though a giant had become weary of arguing and was having a final mutter to himself as he sloped off. We had survived.

The next morning all the headlines in the newspapers told of the terrible storm over Merseyside. The air outside was fresh and the street had been scrubbed clean with the rain. As I got ready for work my heart fell. I discovered I wasn't pregnant after all. I sat in the toilet and cried, looking at the red blood on the pink toilet paper.

Not yet then Matthew, I thought. Not yet, but soon.

A Dandelion By Any Other Name

By late Autumn I was starting to get really worried. James and I were still seeing each other but he didn't seem to be interested in getting married. No matter how many hints I offered, he never mentioned the subject. He seemed such an alien creature. He was eighteen and I was still sixteen.

Time was running out. Brenda Rainer was already married and had a baby. Janet had some sort of a boyfriend who worked in the sausage factory, but she still continued to see Donald now and again, mainly for the chocolate and free car trips. Cushla often went with them. While her little sister was there, Janet was safe.

My mum had totally given up on men. I'd hoped she would remarry and we could change our names in the process, but she seemed to prefer singing about love rather than living it. I warned her she'd end up dying as Lily Rammsbottom and that name would be engraved on her tombstone for evermore, for the whole world to scoff at. 'I don't give a bugger what name's on it,' she said. She had her routine of betting on the horses, going to the bingo twice a week and watching TV. She told us, her growing daughters, that she didn't much mind what we did, as long as we didn't bring any babies back home.

But a baby was part of my plan. Sex was becoming an important feature in my life. At every opportunity, which was at least once a week, I would organise a place for James and me to perform sexual intercourse. It was important for two very good reasons. Firstly, it was a pretty reliable way of becoming pregnant, and if I did fall pregnant, James would have to marry me. Secondly, James really enjoyed it, and for those few moments he was in my power. Each time we copulated I waited for the expected proposal of marriage. After all, he said I was good in bed. It didn't seem to take much effort to be good in bed. All I did was lie there while he did everything, apart from wiping the mess up afterwards. I wondered what other women did, those who weren't good in bed. Out of curiosity I joined the library as Deirdre Robinson and took out a book on sex.

Janet hadn't heard of such things either. Orgasms for women, it said. My mum and Brenda Rainer had told us everything we ever wanted to know about sex, but neither had mentioned this. 'Why didn't yer tell us about orgasms?' I asked my mum, showing her the paragraph in the book.

Sitting in her armchair, with a cup of tea balanced on the black vinyl arm, she began to read about female orgasm, her brow furrowed as her eyes moved along the lines. She put the book face down on her lap, picked up her cup of tea and supped in a moment of contemplation, looking through the net curtains towards the sky, which seemed to be the place where all intelligible human thought materialised. 'Ah, yer don't wanna believe everything yer read in books,' she finally declared. 'That's all daft that is.'

'Why's it in a book then?' Janet asked, not sure if she was missing out on something or not.

My mum picked up the book again, skimming once more over the mysterious paragraph before rationalising that it could only be referring to some strange tribes in Africa, people who were different to us. Maybe the ones with the long necks full of bracelets. It seemed hardly reasonable for an explanation, but as long as I was doing the main bit right – the bit about sperms and eggs – that was all that mattered.

But each month I encountered the same scarlet greeting. I went back to the library and took the book out again. I learnt all about ovulation. My mum confirmed there was indeed such a thing. She knew about ovulation. She had used the Vatican Roulette method before buying a Dutch cap. Cushla was a by-product of it.

A Dandelion By Any Other Name

From Cushla's expression I could tell something had happened. For a start, Janet was sitting in my mum's favourite armchair, the chair nearest to the fire, and my mum was standing over her with a 'what now?' expression on her face. I'd only just come home from work and was expecting to be presented with my tea. Usually egg and chips on a Monday.

'She's pregnant,' Cushla told me, nodding her head towards Janet.

'Yer liar!' I replied, looking at Janet, and knowing from everybody's expression it must be true. There was an initial sense of shocking, delightful envy. Poor awkward thumb-sucking Janet was going to be a mother. Why hadn't she mentioned it to me? I looked at her body, but she looked the same as she always did. 'Is it true?' I asked. My mum nodded a yes.

I now felt sick with jealousy. That should have been me sitting there getting all the special attention. Especially after how hard I'd been trying. But it was Janet who now had that miracle of life growing inside her. A baby. A little person with whom she would experience the greatest love affair of her life. She'd better not call it Matthew, I thought. I asked her if the father was Donald.

'Don't be soft!' she snapped. 'As if I'd go with him.'

In her new state she was more worthy of respect and she knew it. There was something about marriage, being pregnant or being a mother that promoted you up a notch on the social scale. Janet was now positioned as the alpha female while I became the inferior bitch.

She said the father was a lad called Jimmy from the sausage factory, but he had gone away on a ship and didn't know about the baby. My God, I thought, if she didn't find the man and marry him, the baby would be born a Rammsbottom. Had she considered that? Of course she had, but she had options. She had told Donald about her pregnancy and his response was to marry her as soon as possible, and bring the baby up as his own.

'Yer can't marry someone older than yer mother!' I said.

'If I can't get hold of Jimmy Crumb, then I'll have to,' she replied.

Jimmy Crumb! Janet Crumb and baby Crumb! We seemed born to be ridiculed. But the thoughts of marrying Donald with his freckly big hands and rapidly expanding bald patch were too repulsive to contemplate. We had long imagined and discussed what might lurk under his pervert's raincoat, and if Janet married him she would have to find out. He would be my brother-in-law!

But Donald did have a normal name and access to copious amounts of chocolate, which had to count for something in his favour. My mum was very pro-Donald and maintained that Janet could do a lot worse for herself. 'At least he doesn't smoke,' she echoed, advising us how smokers keep you awake at night worrying about burning beds.

After all my mum's threats about bringing babies back home, she didn't seem too concerned about Janet's pregnancy. 'To err is human, to forgive is divine,' she repeated to nobody in particular. I wanted to be in a position to be forgiven too, but James' sperm and my eggs didn't seem interested in each other. Janet had just turned sixteen and I was almost seventeen. I felt the most desperate I'd ever felt in my life, and I suspected Janet did too.

It was one of those beautiful days in April. A Sunday afternoon when the sky was pale blue and a fresh spring breeze caused the clouds to scud along so rapidly that the sun seemed to be turning off and on like an electric light. James and I were walking hand in hand through Derby Park. I was wearing a flimsy, sleeveless dress I'd bought in a winter sale. I'd been waiting for a day such as this to present it to the world. When the sun went behind the clouds, goosepimples appeared on my bare arms, disappearing just as quickly when the sun came out again. The lightness and soft texture of the dress made me feel feminine and attractive.

James stopped walking and sat down on the grass, gently pulling me down with him. He was wearing a white, open-necked shirt with long sleeves. For some reason I always found James wearing a white shirt very alluring. Maybe it was his wavy hair resting on the collar, or maybe I associated white shirts with being middle-class, I don't know.

Lying on the grass I felt strange and daring, full of primitive urges. It was that magical season of spring and everything around us was new and on the move. James gave me a long, slow kiss and then pulled his head back to look at me. The dress made me feel sensuous and enticing. I caressed its soft texture for my own pleasure. When James moved my hair away from my face I felt cosseted, like a little girl. Without speaking he stretched his hand out and picked a bright yellow dandelion from among its sisters in the grass and offered it to me. It was the most romantic and moving thing anybody had ever done for me. We called those flowers peederbeds in Berry Street, but James and probably most other people called them dandelions.

'A dandelion by any other name is still a peederbed,' I said, hoping he would laugh, but he didn't. I accepted the small yellow flower as though it were a bouquet of expensive orchids. He was quiet and continued looking at me with a strange expression. This is it, I thought. He's going to ask me to marry him.

But he didn't. We got up and walked a little further down the path before sitting down on a wooden bench near the children's playground. I still held the dandelion. My heart was almost bursting with frustrated emotion. I couldn't stand the waiting, the passive waiting to be asked. Bending down slowly, I knelt before James as he sat on the bench. My knee was hurting on the gravel, and I felt slightly silly, but I continued anyway. 'James, will yer marry me?' I asked, offering him the same yellow flower. There was a moment's silence while he focused on a couple of children playing on a wooden see-saw and then turned his eyes back to me. 'Will yer, James?' I pleaded. 'Will yer marry me?'

A smile crept across his face.

'You make it very hard for me to say no,' he said.

'Does that mean the answer's yes?' I asked. I could hear my voice quivering with emotion.

'Yes,' he said taking the dandelion. 'I suppose it's about time we got married.'

14

A Celebration

The wedding was set for the end of June, a few weeks after my seventeenth birthday. Not only was I on the verge of a new and normal life, but the man himself was a real catch. He didn't smoke or drink and he didn't beat me up. And those beautiful eyes with luxurious long lashes would be passed on through his genes to my children. Two boys and a girl, I decided. And the sooner the better.

James now knew my surname. He wasn't horrified or shocked when I told him, just slightly amused. He couldn't understand why it was such an abomination to me. Most people couldn't. They had never personally experienced such a life.

James was very much an anti-smoker and while I was with him I didn't smoke. But at work, it was different. Most of the women smoked, and at breaktimes I would light up with them. Our smoking had style. Inhaling was accompanied by an expression of narrow-eyed concentration, and exhaling involved tilting the head back to blow smoke serenely into the air. Even holding a cigarette between two fingers while we talked felt good. It was a stylish displacement activity. I never really enjoyed the physical sensation of inhaling smoke, only the enigmatic, sophisticated image it seemed to portray. Going home on the train, I always sucked a few peppermints to make sure James couldn't detect the forbidden tobacco smell on my breath.

In the weeks leading up to the wedding, James' mother discovered something cataclysmic about her future daughter-in-law. I couldn't cook. I couldn't even boil an egg. The discovery was made one evening when I was invited to tea at James' place. His mother hadn't been exactly overjoyed when her youngest son told her he was getting married. There was no interest in matrimonial details, no questions regarding when or where the event might take place. If something's ignored long enough, maybe it will go away. Mrs Mortimer had been a cook and housekeeper for wealthy people in Wales and was very knowledgable in the practicalities of domestic life.

She was standing in her kitchen wearing a white apron when I arrived. It was only then I learned the horrifying news: I was expected to help her prepare the tea. There were utensils on the kitchen bench I'd never seen before, let alone handled. Things such as colanders and graters, and a sieve. At seventeen years old I was as domesticated as an alley-cat. My mum had never once asked any of her daughters to wash a dish or make a bed, let alone peel a potato. And we were more than happy to remain in blissful ignorance.

But the day of reckoning had come, and when Mrs Mortimer asked me to peel a few potatoes, I couldn't. 'She can't even peel a spud!' I heard her saying to James, pretending humour and lightness but really wanting him to think twice about marrying me. Warning him of the liability he was about to take on. But I was a modern young woman and I knew more than she was giving me credit for. An inability to peel potatoes was not the end of the world, not when you could buy packets of potato powder from the shops. All you had to do was add boiling water from the kettle to the powder and within seconds it became instant mashed potato. No messing about with peeling or watching pans of boiling water. And if James didn't like that, there was always the chippy. Weren't chips fried potatoes? That Mrs Mortimer just wasn't with it.

But she lost all pretence at humour when she realised I didn't know the difference between a cabbage and a lettuce. She asked me to pass her a lettuce from the pantry and I gave her a cabbage instead. It was round and green, so I wasn't really that far off the mark. Not enough for her to tut-tut and ask me where I'd been all my life.

Not sure what to call my future mother-in-law, I addressed her as Mrs Mortimer. I enjoyed the sound of it. Mrs Mortimer – it was soon to be my name, and every night I looked in the mirror and said the words, 'Mrs Mortimer'. I tried them with a serious expression – 'Now look here, Mrs Mortimer'; with a happy-go-lucky expression – 'Oh, Mrs Mortimer! ha, ha, ha'; and with the girls at work – 'Pass us another ciggy will yer, Mrs M.' When I repeated the name over and over very quickly, it began to sound like metamorphosis. How apt, I thought.

Yes, the new name suited me very well. I was so happy, I even opened a couple of boxes of chocolates I'd been hoarding and shared them with my family. My only worry was having to live with the in-laws until we could afford a place of our own. James' father was no problem; he just smiled benignly and watched TV most of the time. But the mother would be a different kettle of fish. I decided to be a passive, good little daughter-in-law, at least until I'd secured what I wanted more than anything in the world, which was her son. And his name officially mine.

Luckily James wasn't too concerned about my lack of culinary skills, or so I thought. I invited him to our house in Berry Street to experience the delights of a Sunday roast, which I would make for him myself. I organised my mum to peel the potatoes, cook them in the roasting dish with the meat, and boil the cabbage. All I had to do was make the gravy. I didn't want to pour the fat over the meal the way my mum did; James might mention it to his mother and she'd be sure to make some sarcastic remark. So I bought a packet of Bisto gravy from the shop. I was really all out to impress my man. Janet and my mum were ushered off to a new spiritualist ('this one's supposed to be really good!') and Cushla was bribed with a box of chocolates and a shilling to spend the afternoon anywhere but at home.

When James arrived, he commented on the delicious smell coming from the kitchen. He hovered about as I took the roasting dish from the oven and began to carve the meat (New Zealand lamb). I felt like a housewife, complete in my natural female state of caring and catering for others. As I was stirring the gravy in a pan on the stove, James picked up the Bisto packet and began reading. 'This isn't proper gravy,' he said with a voice of authority. A voice I'd never heard before.

'It is so!' I answered. I wasn't going to have a man tell me what's what in the kitchen. My dad never ever asked what it was my mum put in front of him; he just ate it with relish and gratitude. We all did.

'Make it the proper way,' James instructed. 'With the meat juices and some flour.'

I wondered what he was talking about. Meat juices? Did he mean the grease that floated around the meat and potatoes like an oily moat? I'd never heard such a euphemistic term for fat! And besides, we didn't have any flour. I was determined to be a modern wife, and my husband was going to have proper Bisto gravy on his

A Dandelion By Any Other Name

Sunday dinner.

'No!' I said 'You can like this or lump it.' Unfortunately the contents of the pan began turning into soft lumps as I spoke. I stirred vigorously.

'Then stuff the dinner, I don't want any of it if you're gonna pour that on it,' he said.

I couldn't believe he was carrying on like this. I told him there was nothing wrong with my gravy and he was just being insulting.

'You do as I tell you,' he ordered. 'If you want to be my wife, you make real gravy.'

My God, I thought, I'm not going to be bossed about by a little country bumpkin. Acting on impulse, I rushed into the living room, pulled a cigarette from the drawer and lit it in front of him. His face turned a deep red. He was livid with fury and told me to put it out immediately. In a terribly theatrical manner I blew the smoke into the air and looked at him with glaring defiance. My mouth sucked hard on the next drag.

'Bitch!' he said as he pulled the cigarette from me and stubbed it out on the saucer containing our holy raw onion. An act of desecration. 'The next one'll go out in your face!' he warned me.

We yelled childish abuse at each other before he stopped me dead in mid-insult. He said the wedding was off and he wanted nothing more to do with me. He stormed out, banging the front door behind him.

What an idiot I was! Instead of being agreeable and nice, I'd allowed myself to be carried away by my own foolish taste for drama. I hadn't even meant to say such things: they just popped out as though I were on stage playing a part. Like those American housewives on TV, arms akimbo yelling back at their husbands. A mouse, that's what I should have been, a nice quiet mouse. The way my mum was with my dad. It even says it in the Bible:

Woman, be a mouse, do what your husband tells you because he is over you just as Jesus is over the church. That's what it says all right. That's the message.

My pathetic impulses! To lose a life over gravy.

In the kitchen the gravy had been left bubbling away on the stove. It was now just one big burnt lump, like me. I plopped it into the sink and ran tap water over it until it disintegrated down the drain. I splashed my face with cold water to try and curb the chin-puckering that was starting up. Picking up the leg of roast lamb I pushed my face into it like a wild animal. Tearing at it with my teeth and squeezing my tongue down the bone to get at the hot marrow. I allowed the grease to smear my face, eating like a primitive cave-woman. And it was definitely greasy, fatty meat grease, not meat juices. I did leave some dinner for my mum and sisters. Not much meat, but plenty of potatoes and cabbage.

So the wedding was off. With a sulking heavy regret I went upstairs to bed and put my head under the blankets. I could smell James' body smell on the sheets. It conjured up babies. Cherubic little boys with fat baby fingers touching their mammy's face. I ached for that touch with a primitive lust.

Janet's pregnancy was developing nicely. She hadn't had much luck trying to track down Jimmy Crumb, and Donald was now becoming a constant nuisance. He took her out to cafés for her tea. As well as the usual supply of chocolate, he also bought her presents. He was desperate to marry her and bring the baby up as his own.

'Imagine him on top of yer – "Jean, oh Jesus! Jean!"' I teased with closed eyes and a gyrating pelvis, 'with his freckly fingernails and green gingery breath all down yer neck.'

Janet told me to shut up. She didn't fancy Donald but she was pregnant and she had a surname that nobody could possibly allow a child to be born with. She would give Jimmy another few weeks to turn up. If there was still no word from him by the time she was into her eighth month, there was no alternative but to marry Donald.

But her luck changed. All our luck changed. Very suddenly and from a most unexpected quarter. Janet found out that anybody could change their name by a thing called a deed poll. You just paid a solicitor some money, signed a form, and from then on you could be whatever name you chose. It was part of the law. A great feeling of release washed over us as we decided on new names for ourselves. Janet liked the sound of Jones. If the baby was a boy, he would be Michael Jones; a baby girl would be Angela Jones. Nothing to fear from those names. They sounded ordinary and nondescript – an impenetrable fortress against harassment.

Janet made an appointment with a solicitor for the following Thursday. She said we could call her JJ. But my mum complained, saying Janet was wasting money changing her name when a perfectly good man was willing to marry her. According to my mum, love and marriage didn't necessarily go together like a horse and carriage. 'Here's him with a house in Seaforth and a good job, yer might as well take him,' my mum advised, 'or someone else'll snap him up. A good mug like him.' She always referred to Donald as 'him'.

'You have him if yer think he's that good,' Janet would reply to my mum. 'He's more your age anyway.'

My mum tried to explain the obvious. Donald only wanted Janet, and besides, older men are better prospects than younger ones. For a start they have more money and they die sooner. 'Yer could do a lot worse than him,' she concluded, heading into the kitchen to fill the kettle.

I told my family that I too had decided to change my name by deed poll, and that I now wouldn't be marrying James. They didn't seem too surprised. No questions were asked, no lies were given. The lack of interest wasn't a form of politeness to spare my feelings; it was simply indifference.

As nobody else had bothered to make any sort of wedding plans, nobody was particularly put out. I'd bought a wedding dress and veil, and organised James to see the vicar at the youth club to arrange a Saturday afternoon wedding for the end of June. We had both been to a jewellery shop to measure up for wedding rings. As far as planning a wedding was concerned, that was it. There had been some muttering about my sisters being bridesmaids, but the idea had never developed past the muttering stage. Besides, Janet was now too pregnant to be a bridesmaid. She had also been more concerned about who exactly might be at her own wedding, placing a ring on her finger.

I decided to make an appointment with a solicitor myself to purchase a nice ordinary name. Perhaps Jackson or Wilson. They seemed so perfect compared to Rammsbottom. Cushla also wanted to change her name. She wanted something a bit more interesting, such as Van der Haven. 'Someone might ask if yer father's foreign with a name like that,' I warned her. But she was quite happy to say yes, her father was a Dutch captain. I liked Cushla for saying things like that. She was rebellious and didn't mind how she upset other people's expectations.

I felt so happy for us all that day, sitting together in the living room. I wished we could celebrate our long-awaited release with champagne or something special. Anything but tea, which was all we ever seemed to drink. When I mentioned wanting to celebrate with something stronger than PG Tips, my mum pulled an unopened bottle of gin from the kitchen cabinet. She'd won it on the bingo a few weeks before and had put it away for Christmas.

A Dandelion By Any Other Name

Even Cushla wanted to try a glass of it. The trouble was, we had nothing to drink it with – no orange juice or lemonade.

Bringing four little glasses from the cabinet in the front parlour, I set them out on the table, opened the gin and poured. The glasses had small pictures painted on them: men on horses blowing horns and beagle dogs off on a hunt. They also had been won on the bingo and were being used for the first time. We sniffed at the gin before trying it, giggling like excited children.

'Well, down the hatch,' my mum said, holding the glass up and then knocking it back like they did in cowboy films. We all copied her and after a few seconds of silence, the coughing and spluttering began. I could feel the heat from the alcohol going down my gullet, burning the back of my throat.

My mum was smacking and licking her lips. I could tell from the shine in her eyes she was starting to enjoy herself. And I was too. It was a tremendous feeling being part of that little female family, swigging away like uncouth dockers. 'Let's have another,' I suggested, going around filling the empty glasses. Nobody resisted the offer.

'Rammsbottoms up!' I said lifting my glass and my arse in the air. They all laughed. I could make fun of that name now it was going. Cushla screwed her face up as she swallowed her second drink. 'Yer not cryin' already are yer?' I said. 'Here, have some more, yer'll start gettin' used to the taste.' Cushla lifted her empty glass for another drink, still grimacing from the last one.

My mum seemed to be torn between continuing to have a good time with her daughters and making a stand against it. She chose to enjoy herself. We loved seeing my mum laughing. She would close her eyes and shake her shoulders when she was having a good laugh. It was contagious.

I wanted to keep the laughing going so I performed my

impersonation of Donald making love to Janet. It went down well. Then Cushla pretended to be Brother Roy in the fruit shop, speaking just as he did in a slow Yorkshire accent. 'Come and see what a fine big turnip I have here Janet, have you ever seen the likes?' We roared laughing. Cushla was only twelve but she knew the type of humour her family appreciated.

Janet remained seated in the armchair, quietly enjoying herself but somehow managing to remain aloof. She was being sensible, making the rest of us feel wild and uncouth in comparison. She was a spectator rather than a performer, and with seven months' pregnancy under her dress, she sat proudly in my mum's armchair like a queen on a throne.

By the fourth round my mum was starting to sing 'Come Back Paddy Riley' with tears in her eyes. 'Let's sing something a bit more lively,' I complained. Cushla started singing 'Summer Holiday', which was still banned from the household. Singing to drown her out, I began the Beatles song 'When I Saw Her Standing There'. The cacophony made by three people all singing different songs was dreadful.

My mum was the first to stop, her crying turned to laughing. But Janet stopped us all as she leaned forward to throw up into the fire-grate. 'Yer could've done it in the bucket outside,' moaned Cushla, holding her nose against the smell of vomit.

My mum finally put the top on the gin. I placed some old newspapers over the vomit as Janet lay back in the armchair panting. She blamed our singing for making her sick. 'A Cliff Richard song would make anyone sick,' I said, finishing off the last of my gin.

My mum brought us each a cup of tea, serving Janet first. I looked at Janet and decided she really would suit the name Jones. A fresh burst of joy filled my heart as I remembered again the marvel of the deed poll. It was as though we'd won a huge sum of money on the football pools and a better new life was about to begin. I was happy that my new little nephew or niece was going to get a good start in life – the name Jones instead of the monstrosity that dare not speak its name. And not having to marry Donald Campbell was a huge relief for Janet.

'You'll be the only Bottom left among us' I said to my mum. 'Why don't you change too – go back to being Lily Patterson or something?'

'What's in a name?' she quoted, hoping to sound philosophical but not getting anywhere. Then it must have dawned on her that we could end up a household of different surnames, and none of us with a husband. I had chosen Wilson, Janet was to be Jones and Cushla definitely liked the sound of Van der Haven. And of course there was Lily Rammsbottom too. 'What the hell will the fuckin' postman think?' my mum wondered aloud. We all started the laughing again. There was nothing more funny than somebody who didn't usually swear saying the word fuck, especially after a few drinks. My mum enjoyed the applause, laughing more than any of us.

'He's paid to deliver letters, not to think,' I said, remembering the nosy little postman who had put a stop to my autograph business a few years before.

Cushla was already scribbling out the Rammsbottom on her school bag and writing Van der Haven instead. 'Yer can't do that!' said my mum. But Cushla continued writing her new Dutch name in big black scrawl. CUSHLA VAN DER HAVEN. I encouraged her, saying it had a certain something. The sound of a TV celebrity, or perhaps a model.

But poor Cushla wasn't allowed to change her name. Being only twelve years old she needed parental consent, and my mum said she wouldn't pay when there would soon be plenty of fellows around willing to marry her. I think she must have meant 'him'. Poor old Donald. Nobody else seemed very interested in us.

It was about two o'clock on the following Saturday afternoon that he came over to our house – James Mortimer, the fellow with very strong feelings on gravy. 'Wanna come for a walk?' he asked, his eyes darting about at the ground, avoiding contact with mine. We walked in silence to Derby Park. Twice he took his hand from his pocket and let it hang at his side, hoping I would hold it as I used to. But I didn't. All the feelings of desperation had gone.

In the park, we sat on a bench. He was obviously feeling awkward but at last he managed to say what was on his mind. 'I'm sorry,' he whispered, still looking down rather than at me. I pretended not to hear so he would have to say it again, louder. 'I'm sorry,' he repeated, 'about what happened last Sunday.' I wanted to make him suffer more by not acknowledging the apology, but when I saw those feathery eyelashes and the fair hair curling under his ear, my heart softened and I kissed him gently on the cheek.

'I'm sorry too, James. I never meant to say all those horrible things.' We cuddled together on the bench for a few minutes, neither of us saying anything. I loved the smell of him, the touch of his body against mine.

'I still want to marry you,' he said. 'Do you still want me?' Did I still want him when I could be Deirdre Wilson the following week? Of course I did. Every cell in my body was now crying out for a baby.

'What if I poured Bisto on yer dinner?' I said, trying him out.

He smiled and said Bisto would be fine. 'But one thing I would ask,' he said, 'and that is you don't smoke.' I agreed to that. I never liked smoking anyway, it was just the look of it – that Humphrey Bogart look of being in charge of yourself.

'I've got something for you,' he said shyly, reaching into his pocket. It was the squashed dandelion, a common little weed that had become our special flower.

'It's still lovely' I said. And it really was. A bright yellow star.

James then took something else from his pocket and placed it in my hand. It was a little red velvet box containing a solitaire diamond engagement ring. I'd never expected such a thing and felt totally undeserving of it. It sparkled in the sunlight as I awkwardly placed it on the appropriate finger. It fitted perfectly. For this man, I decided, I would be a mouse. A mousy, perfect little wife. A wife interested in gardening and even making gravy with flour and meat juices.

And to help me maintain my mousy aspirations, I would once again turn to Christianity.

We walked home hand in hand, hardly speaking. Every now and then I lifted our coupled hands to my mouth and kissed his knuckles. Feelings of tenderness and love overflowed but could not be verbalised. I decided to continue using my own name for a few more weeks rather than change it by deed poll. It would make the wedding even more precious.

I was now an engaged woman. I had a fiancée. At last somebody was willing to marry me and make a normal person of me. To be normal and ordinary was all I'd ever craved. To have on my marble tombstone (made by my husband James) an epitaph that would read: 'Here lie the remains of Deirdre Mortimer, an ordinary person who lived an ordinary life.' But it's the extraordinary that happens to you while you're busy planning something more mundane.

15

Guys and Jokers

Janet Jones gave birth to a little boy she called Michael. Her old admirer, Donald, hovered about in hope for a few months before finally realising she would never marry him.

But I did marry James. The Saturday afternoon wedding saw me emerge from the church the happiest I had ever felt in my life. The joyful pealing of Christ Church bells tolled in the new me – Mrs Deirdre Mortimer. The awful maiden name was cast off like the dead skin of a snake, and discarded at the altar. That night, my wedding night, I crossed off the number one goal written in my diary. It was time to concentrate on goal number two: babies.

If James had never felt like a stud before, he certainly did for the few years following the marriage. We were living with James' parents, but most of our time was spent either at work or in bed. Straight after tea each evening, I would signal James by slowly raising my eyes towards the ceiling, towards our bedroom. Leaving his mother to clean up the dishes alone, we would skulk upstairs for our early evening lovemaking. There was no caring how much the bed banged against the wall; it was all for a good cause. I could imagine James' mother tut-tutting at her grinning husband as they listened to the repetitious hammering from the room above, shaking her head in disappointment at her son's choice of a wife.

But in spite of the copious sexual activity there was still no baby. We were saving our wages towards a deposit for a house – at least I was. All my desires centred around building a nest for our future babies. And a dog, and a cat. I blamed James' mother for my apparent infertility. Having to live with disapproving in-laws seemed the most likely cause.

I didn't even know James had been making inquiries. Special letters began arriving in the mail. Application forms for emigration to South Africa, Canada, Australia and New Zealand. The first country to accept us was where he decided we would go. While I dreamed of building nests, he was wanting to fly.

But I was now Mrs Mortimer and enjoying the normality of a meaningless surname. Everyday little things such as filling in a form became a pleasant experience. Having my name called out in the doctor's waiting-room filled me with a newly found pride. I didn't feel any need or desire to live in an alien land. I was happy enough in my own home town.

James accused me of being selfish. He was restless living in Bootle, calling it a dump. With the amount of sex he'd been enjoying it was surprising there was any energy left for restlessness! When the acceptance letter from New Zealand House arrived, he tried to persuade me that life 'down under' would have more to offer than a place like Bootle. 'Think of the opportunities for our kids,' he pleaded, knowing full well my vulnerabilities on that subject.

I had never imagined myself as an immigrant. The word only ever conjured up brown-skinned people in turbans and saris. But I remembered my premarital affirmation to be a good mousy little wife, and so I agreed. We would pack up all our meagre possessions and emigrate.

On a warm Sunday evening in August, we said farewell to our friends and relatives. Janet felt too sick to see me off, but Cushla and my mum were there to wave goodbye as the train pulled out of Lime Street station for London. Quietly smiling, I waved back at them. I was glad Janet couldn't come. It was painful enough.

Although evening, it was still light as the train rattled slowly past all the old brick buildings of Liverpool. It was like watching a black-and-white film in slow motion, something from the previous century. I felt as though I was leaving my own soul. It didn't seem to matter whether we were journeying to the North Pole or to the moon. I was a reluctant adventurer.

I felt devastated. My eyes welled with tears and no amount of rationalising or control could stop the weeping. James was becoming annoyed. For him it was the beginning of a great adventure, an opportunity to start afresh in a new country, and already his wife was spoiling it all.

I had never travelled as far away as London before, but there were over 12,000 miles to go from there. I wondered if I would ever see my family again, or Janet's son, my little nephew Michael. I would never be there to see him grow up. Each hour of travelling was taking me further and further away, not only in distance, but in time. When we reached Heathrow, my eyes and face were red and puffy with crying. We lifted our suitcases containing all our wordly goods onto the check-in scales, and received two boarding passes for a flight to Los Angeles, and from there on to New Zealand. The antipodes.

The thing that strikes you most about New Zealand is how bright the sky is. Even on an overcast day the glare can make your eyes squint for protection. Tony Clark, the man who had sponsored James, helped us find a small, furnished house to rent in Torbay on Auckland's North Shore. He said nearly all the Poms liked to live on the Shore but didn't know why. Maybe the names of the towns such as Browns Bay, Torbay and Long Bay had an English seaside sound to them, so the 'Poms' could feel perpetually on holiday. There was a 'dairy' over the road from our house where we stocked up on bread, butter, milk and tea – the basics for survival. It seemed strange buying the same New Zealand butter I'd bought in supermarkets in England. It was a small familiarity, but it cheered me enormously.

It was in the middle of the afternoon that it hit us: jetlag. It was as though somebody had drugged our tea, and even with all the new and interesting things around us we started to physically dissolve. We lay on the bed, fully clothed, covered ourselves with a blanket (made of pure New Zealand wool), and slept. At 3am we were wide awake, opening our suitcases and settling into our new home. There was a bathroom with two taps over a pink sparkling bath. I turned the tap labelled 'hot' and warm water poured out. It was the most luxurious bath I'd ever had. Far better than the cockroach-infested public baths of Bootle, far better than our plastic bowl in Berry Street.

Although we found the cold wind and rain disappointing, I couldn't believe how beautiful all the Auckland houses were. All detached with gardens back and front. Our two-bedroomed home was no exception. The fully fenced back garden conjured up one immediate image for me – a dog. If we could just have a dog, it would be like having some sort of a relative. Some extension of ourselves. James said we shouldn't rush things – buying a dog on our second day in New Zealand might be a bit foolish. But he was pleased to see his wife perking up. After a twelve-hour sleep I had lost that puffy-eyed melancholic look of the chronically depressed. New Zealand wasn't so bad.

For our first weekend, James' new boss Tony introduced us to one of New Zealand's most popular sports – rugby. He called it football, but when we stood at the sidelines watching the game, it slowly dawned on me that this football was different. I'd never seen Liverpool or Everton footballers carrying the ball in their arms. I was intrigued.

There were other differences we encountered that weekend. Men were referred to as 'guys' or 'jokers'. If something was good, it was 'beaut', and people 'shouted' you a drink. The Kiwi accent itself took a bit of getting used to. When Tony asked if he could borrow a pen, he must have wondered why such a simple request required so much fumbling about in a small purse. And I was wondering why he needed a pin.

On the Saturday evening, Tony and his wife, Sylvia, took us to an after-rugby party. It was held in a cold community hall somewhere in Point Chevalier, where the Clarks lived. There were people walking to and fro, carrying large jugs of beer. I was seated among the Kiwi womenfolk, while Tony introduced James to the male counterparts. The men seemed to instinctively form themselves in circles, each with their right hand holding a glass of beer and their left hand in their pockets. They all stood with their legs slightly apart as they talked and laughed loudly. I could see from James' posture that he was really trying to fit in, trying to be one of the guys. But they were talking rugby, a subject James knew little about.

The women mainly talked about their children, about a thing called a Plunket which I presumed to be some sort of a dessert, and about their gardens. I hoped I too would soon be able to talk about my children.

Stepping outside to get away from the smokey atmosphere, I noticed Tony follow me. He was tall, with a rugby player's build. I couldn't help admiring his dark wavy hair and 'come to bed' eyes, which were surrounded by thick dark lashes. It wasn't fair how all the men seemed to have the long eyelashes while I had to enhance my stubble as best I could with mascara.

'Enjoying yourself?' he asked.

'Yeah, it's great,' I lied. 'Thanks for bringin' us.'

He moved his muscular body closer to mine, as though waiting to be embraced. As though it would be impossible for me to resist. But I turned away.

'What's the matter?'

'Nothink,' I said. 'I'm just cold, that's all.' It was the worst thing I could have said, as he put his arms around my shoulders.

'I know how to warm you up.'

I was about to tell him to get lost, but I remembered he was James' new boss. It would be a bad start for us if I upset him. I was saved from any further embarrassment when the door swung open by a couple leaving the hall to go home. I quickly walked back inside and took my seat among the women.

Sylvia Clark was short and slim, with blond hair cut in an attractive page-boy style. She really looked like a Sylvia. We had eaten tea at their home before coming to the party, and I was greatly impressed with her cooking ability. She had made the tomato soup herself, from a recipe book, as well as the chocolate gateaux for dessert. I felt a little intimidated, but enjoyed the food anyway. I couldn't understand her husband leching after me when he had such a talented and attractive wife.

At about ten o'clock, I asked James if we could go home. Tony and Sylvia insisted on us going back to their place to stay the night, but I politely refused, saying I needed my pills, and unfortunately I'd left them at home.

'What pills are they?' asked James.

'Yer know,' I assured him. 'Me pills I have to take.' He didn't know about my pills because they didn't exist. But the alarming thought of what might happen if we went back to the Clarks' place did exist. We caught a taxi back to Torbay.

To prove I wasn't a secret schizophrenic or worse, I took two aspirins from the bathroom cabinet and swallowed them with a glass of water in front of James. 'Headache,' I explained.

'Well I'm feeling really knackered. It's been a long day,' he said, climbing into bed still wearing his socks and underpants. But knackered or not, he would have to perform his marital duty before going to sleep. There were babies waiting to be created.

I knew I'd become a Kiwi when I couldn't eat my morning toast without the accompanying Vegemite. I'd also discovered another delicious new taste: roast kumera.

Because there was so much novelty in almost everything around us, a feeling of euphoria soon developed for our new country. Little things such as waiting for the buzzer to sound before crossing a road, wheeling trolleys around in a supermarket, and mowing lawns every second week. It was all so new, with almost an American feel to it. I copied the women shoppers in Three Guys supermarket, lifting the egg-carton lids and carefully checking the eggs, or 'iggs' as they seemed to pronounce it, before placing them in the trolley. I wasn't sure what I was looking for; cracks I suppose.

Summer was not far off and each day James and I became more certain that New Zealand really was what people called it – Godzone. Being Deirdre Mortimer in Godzone, nobody guessed at the past absurdity of Rammsbottom. Only my Liverpudlian accent now differentiated me from others. Many people thought I was Scottish or Welsh, and I was happy for them to think that. It seemed one up on being a Pom anyway.

James was given a van as part of his job at Clarks marble firm, and our weekends were spent driving to some of Auckland's most scenic places. I fell in love with the wildness of the west coast, places such as Muriwai and Whatapu. The black glittering sand was yet another novelty. Photographs of spectacular coastal scenery were proudly sent back to our relatives in England. I also made James take photos of me showing off the bathroom and toilet, not to mention the garden. To prove to them all we had really hit the jackpot!

Coming from Wales, James had always been an outdoorsy type of person, and New Zealand suited his inclinations perfectly. He bought a fishing rod, a surfcaster he called it, and joined a fishing club. I accompanied him once on a fishing expedition, and he vowed never again. I felt too much empathy for innocent suffering things, and pleaded for the life to be spared of every fish he so enthusiastically pulled ashore. He also booked a proper camping holiday for us in February, when he would be allowed a week's leave. I had never been camping before and wondered if I would survive such a thing.

Near the end of September, the sweet smell of wild jasmine wafted on the warm breezes, heralding in the New Zealand springtime. I sat on our backsteps contemplating all the new little daisies on the lawn and decided it was time for our dog.

Sometimes things are never as bad as you imagine they'll be. Paying a visit to the Auckland Dog Pound was ten times worse. We weren't sure what type of dog we wanted; it was a bit like looking for a house. A case of you'll know it when you see it. But what we saw was heartbreaking. In semi-darkness we walked past a row of small barred prison cells containing a variety of dogs. It was freezing cold. The concrete floor was wet with hosing, and the noise from the dogs was nightmarish. They barked, howled and jumped at the bars for attention, recognising in us a potential deliverance. A small yappy terrier was continually snapped at by a large black labrador as both dogs vied for attention. Every step deeper into this canine Hades became more unbearable. Balancing on their hind legs, each dog focused their hopeful brown eyes on us, while their front paws tried to reach us through the bars. A variety of wagging tails told of hope, each dog desperately pleading 'Choose me!' There was one young Alsation bitch sitting on her own in the background while her fellow inmates clawed and howled. She seemed to have given up all hope as she didn't attempt any marketing of herself.

We learnt that most of the dogs we were looking at were to be put down. No owners had made any inquiries about them for over a week, and unless somebody made an adoption, there was no hope. In tears, I asked James to get us out of there. He was upset too. Walking down Death Row for dogs was not a pleasant experience.

Outside in the van we talked. We had the power to save the life of one of those dogs. The problem was trying to choose. I wanted to take them all. It was like walking through a concentration camp for children and choosing only one to be saved. The Alsation bitch sitting passively in the background? We decided to make inquiries about her.

I couldn't walk past the cells again, so we asked the attendant to bring us the dog to look at. A few minutes later, a woman in a boiler-suit appeared with the Alsation on a lead. This dog was on tomorrow's list to be destroyed. She was approximately eight months old, but there was no sense of play or *joie de vivre* about her. I shuddered to think what she might have already gone through in her young life. James and I both decided simultaneously that she was the one. Our dog.

While we were signing forms and paying the fee, I asked the attendant how she could work in such a place, with so much canine misery to contend with every day. Putting all those lovely innocent dogs to death. Without even looking up from her writing, she said, 'Oh they'll be back'.

'What do you mean?' I asked.

'Reincarnation,' she explained. 'They'll be back.'

I suppose she had to have some sort of comforting philosophy to stay in such a job. Outside we lifted our new dog into the van and headed back over the Harbour Bridge. I studied her face carefully and decided there was only one name she could possibly have. Lucy.

It took a few weeks before Lucy began to trust humans again. We weren't sure what unspeakable cruelty she had suffered, mentally or physically, but there were clues. If either James or I picked up a broom, she cowered pathetically. With lots of kindness and companionship Lucy came back to life. She slept on a rug next to our bed, and each morning I woke to the delights of a wet dog-nose nuzzling my hand. She seemed eternally grateful towards us, and I felt equally as grateful to have the pet of my dreams.

The warm sunny days of November brought more new experiences. Tony and Sylvia took us sailing around the Hauraki Gulf on their yacht. We sailed to Waiheke Island for a lunch of oysters *au naturel* and Chardonnay. I'd never seen oysters before, nor had I ever tasted dry white wine. James loved it all. All he could talk about was buying a boat. But I hadn't inherited my father's seafaring genes. The movement of the boat made me seasick, and the glistening oysters sitting in their craggy shells was not an aesthetically appealing sight.

Sylvia, or Sylv, as Tony called her, gave me a couple of seasickness pills. It must have been the drowsiness caused by the pills that took my mind off the seasickness. But it didn't take my mind off the fact that Tony was up to his old tricks again. While James, Sylvia and little Jason Clark were in the cockpit, Tony sat me down in the saloon and began to massage my neck. He said it was good for seasickness, a kind of natural therapy. But the massaging seemed to have more of a sexual nature to it, and soon he was touching my hair like a lover.

I wondered how many other women he'd done this to, with his wife only a few feet away. He probably thought I was terribly impressed with his yacht and oysters, but they had only succeeded in making me feel nauseous. And he was beginning to have the same sickening effect. He was attractive and intelligent, but the presumption of it all was a big turn-off. He could see his timing wasn't exactly perfect, so he gave me his card – as though I were a potential client. He said he'd ring me up some time, maybe we could go out for lunch or something. Foolishly I felt a little flattered that a wealthy, successful businessman such as Tony could show any interest in me.

Never far from my thoughts, I remembered my quest for a baby. James and I didn't seem to have much luck in that department. James could even be sterile for all I knew. But I knew Tony wasn't. Jason was his four-year-old son and the child was the image of his handsome father. Putting the card in my pocket, I clambered outside to join the others. I was a married woman and I had just been propositioned by a married man.

They say a real optimist is somebody who sees opportunities in all things. I was quickly becoming more optimistic as the day wore on. By the time we said goodbye to Tony and Sylvia I had made my mind up. An extra-marital affair was in order.

16

Home Sickness

If you walk down Clyde Road in Browns Bay you'll catch a glimpse of the sea between the shops. Even on the windiest of days this sea doesn't seem to smell right. Its surrounding scenery is beautiful, with Rangitoto's dominating peak and Rakino Island in the distance. But this sea, which is really the Pacific Ocean, doesn't have that briny maritime smell I associate with saltwater. And no matter how much I sniffed at the air, I was disappointed. Gradually it dawned on me what the problem was: I was beginning to miss the smell of the Mersey, the smell of home.

It was on Christmas day I felt the first real pangs of homesickness. The roast potatoes and turkey looked pathetically out of place as the hot sun poured into the dining room. James and I wore paper hats from the Christmas crackers and wished each other a merry Christmas. There was a strange quietness about the day. We had no relatives to pop in for a sherry or a mince pie, and no presents to give or receive. We had decided not to buy each other presents to save the money, but any little wrapped something would have made a difference to the atmosphere.

Lucy sat next to the table, her eyes concentrating on each

forkful of food we ate. Every now and again a small whimper would escape, reminding us of her presence. I quickly twisted a whole leg off the side of the turkey. 'Happy Christmas, Lucy,' I said, placing the turkey leg in her mouth.

'Don't waste good meat!' cried James, as Lucy took off outside with her present.

I banged my knife and fork down on the plate and wiped my hands on the red and green serviette.

'What's wrong with you?' asked James.

'Everything!' I answered. 'It's night-time in England and it's day-time here. It's snowin' back home, and it's boilin' here. We're upside down on the planet!'

'I'd rather have the sun than the snow,' said James, helping himself to more stuffing. 'And so would you.'

For the first time in months, hot tears filled my eyes and rolled down my cheeks. James softened, and put his arm round me. 'Come on love, cheer up. It's Christmas day.' But that was the problem, it was Christmas day. 'What is it that's really upsetting you?' he asked, wiping away my tears with a crumpled Christmassy serviette.

'It's the turkey,' I replied, looking at the remains of the cooked bird on the table. 'I feel sorry for the poor turkey.'

James sighed and left the table to look again at some brochures he had on boats. Although the turkey looked well and truly out of its misery, it had once been a happy and simple pecking creature. Things just didn't seem fair.

Each month I looked forward to finding myself pregnant, but it didn't happen. It was wonderful having Lucy; she was a loyal and amusing companion, but she was a dog. More than ever I was desperate to start a family, to surround myself with my own children. The thought of cheating on James was repugnant, but maternal longing is stronger than any other desire in the world, even stronger than wifely faithfulness.

Tony finally rang me regarding the promised lunch. I told him to hold on while I checked my diary. But it wasn't a diary I was checking, it was my ovulation chart. I couldn't make it this week, I told him, but Wednesday next week would be perfect.

In the middle of the night I could feel James' warm body next to mine, and a feeling of self-loathing came over me. There always seemed to be something outside of my control dictating my actions. Just as the embarrassing maiden name had caused me to tell so many lies, this inability to become pregnant was now causing me to betray my husband. 'Who can find a virtuous woman? / for her price is far above rubies.' But it had to be done. I couldn't not have children.

Smack in the middle of my ovulation cycle I met Tony for lunch. It was a fancy little restaurant in Takapuna, overlooking the sea. He ordered a bottle of champagne and a dozen oysters for starters. I gazed reluctantly at the oysters, which seemed to smell vaguely of semen.

'Go on, try one,' said Tony, lifting a shell towards my mouth. 'They're supposed to be aphrodisiacs, make you feel sexy.' The icy raw oyster slithered down my throat, leaving a bitter taste in my mouth. I washed it further down with a mouthful of champagne. I let Tony eat the rest of them. For the afternoon I had in mind it was he who would need sexual stamina, not me.

By the time a dessert called Devil's Foodcake arrived I was starting to feel pretty good. Champagne had made me bold. The dessert was very rich and Tony couldn't finish it, but I finished mine, and his too. When it came to tackling anything chocolatey, I was no novice.

They say there is no such thing as a free lunch. But I didn't contribute any money for the lunch, nor towards the motel afterwards; and at the motel it was Tony who would be paying again in a different way.

He was surprisingly hairy. Compared to my smooth-bodied James he was like a gorilla. I noticed his penis was different too. Not only was it bigger, it was circumcised. I took my clothes off and we lay on the orange candlewick bedspread. Tony began to kiss my body. I'd never been kissed by anybody with a moustache before. It felt tickly. Regardless of the moustache, I didn't feel any magic between us, as I did with James. Although all the equipment was there for baby-making, my usual sense of awe was missing. He was so unusually hairy (even on his shoulders and back) it was like committing bestiality.

Also unlike James, he was intent on making sure I had orgasms. But I wasn't there for erotica, my sole concern was procreation. Becoming impatient, I pretended to climax so he would get on with the job. It was as if Tony's concern for my sexual fulfilment was more for his own ego, to prove to himself that he could really satisfy any woman.

At last he finished the task he had been chosen to do. I lay on my back for a while with my knees in the air. I had read somewhere that this gives the sperm a better chance of reaching the egg. Tony lit a cigarette and made a couple of coffees.

'Do yer feel mean cheatin' on yer wife?' I asked him. He only smiled. 'Well, do yer?' I persisted.

'Do you feel mean cheating on James?' he retorted.

'Yeah, I do.'

The conversation stopped there. Although I'd just had sex with Tony I didn't particularly like him. Everything in life seemed to come easily to him. Money, women, big boat, big cock. Life had not kicked him about much, had not moulded him into anything other than a superficial macho image of the successful man, complete with moustache. It wasn't surprising to find out he had inherited his business from his father. It was no rags-to-riches story for Tony.

After the coffee it was obvious he was interested in a second helping, but I decided an extra donation was no longer required. I didn't want to disturb any activity between eggs and sperm currently going on inside me. That night I told James I loved him. He slept soundly in blissful ignorance of his wife's infidelity. I'd betrayed him physically, but I felt in my heart that I'd remained faithful.

Tony rang me again a few days later, but was told sorry, I was fully booked for almost a month. Calculating my chart I told him I could see him in twenty-three days' time. He probably thought I lived on champagne lunches!

But Tony's seeds fell on stony ground. I didn't get pregnant and I decided not to see him again. I'd given him a good go, right in the middle of ovulation, and that was all he was getting. Emigration was now blamed for my inability to conceive. Maybe it was time to go back to England.

The immigrants' honeymoon stage really ended when some photos arrived from my family. Pictures of Janet and little Michael, Cushla and my mum. Michael had large hazel eyes and blond curly hair. I gazed at the photos and cried great sobs of grief. Hearing Rod Stewart's 'Sailing' on the radio only contributed more tears. I put the photos away and turned the radio off. But the feelings of heartache and displacement continued.

James still loved living in the new country. He didn't seem to grieve for his old home as I did. In fact he never gave it a thought.

He was too caught up in buying a tent and preparing for the Great Outdoors, sending me into town to buy tent pegs and sleeping bags from a camping store. When I asked the assistant for tent pegs, she looked at me strangely and told me I could buy them in the chemist shop across the road. The Kiwi accent, which I had found quaint and amusing, now became annoying. I walked out feeling insulted that somebody could think me stupid enough to ask for sanitary protection in a camping store. James thought the story was hilarious, but I was suffering from feelings of helplessness and withdrawal, classic symptoms of culture shock.

To cheer me up, James drove us to Muriwai for a long evening walk with Lucy on the beach. I looked out across the Tasman Sea. The next bit of land out there was Australia. The magnificent untamed grandeur and vastness of Auckland's west coast was awe-inspiring. The old affection and admiration for New Zealand stirred back to life within me.

We sat and watched the sun set on the horizon. The gold sphere of fire slowly disappeared into the sea and a bright green light flashed a final goodbye to the day. The sun was now off to the Northern Hemisphere. Off to England to wake up Janet and Cushla from their winter morning sleep. My heart became heavy again with the pain of separation. But I feigned cheerfulness as much as I could for James' sake. On the drive home, we decided for a number of good reasons, the time had come for me to find a job.

The advertisement said 'Ladies required to train as masseuses, decent women only please.' It sounded to me like an opportunity to train in physiotherapy, or something similar. It couldn't be seedy if only decent women were required. Anyway, there wasn't anything else in the Situations Vacant that I could do. No insurance clerks were wanted. I rang the number and tried to disguise my accent as best I could.

'Are you under twenty-six love?' inquired the male voice at the other end. I said I was. 'What size is your bust?' I wasn't sure. Size 34B bra, I told him. 'Ooh, a bit on the small side, but it might be all right.'

I wondered about the adjective used in the advertisement – decent. Things weren't sounding very decent.

'Have you got wheels love?' This question really threw me. Weals? From whippings?

'What d'yer mean?' I asked.

'Have you got your own car?' I didn't. 'Sorry love, you need your own set of wheels for this job.' He slammed the phone down in my ear. I was glad. I no longer wanted to be a masseuse, decent or not.

The job I eventually got was as a clerical assistant in a medical centre. Working in an office with four other women soon took my mind off homesickness as I settled into a new routine. Mary, Pam, Jan and Barbara were good fun to work with. They frequently used words such as 'neat' or 'grouse' to express approval. A couple of them were keen followers of *Coronation Street* and they all loved reading articles on the British royal family. I'd found a new niche.

Like most Kiwi women, my colleagues were wonderful cooks, and they introduced me to the delicious new world of home baking. They made all their own cakes and biscuits, and every Friday each one in turn would bring in the Friday Treat. They gave me dozens of recipes, and finally I too became hooked. I made everything – banana cakes, cheesecakes, chocolate rough slice with peppermint icing, rum truffles, Pavlova, lemon meringue pie, apple sponge puddings and chocolate ice-cream balls. James loved to see me mixing and rolling things around in the kitchen every weekend. All the baking and consequent eating transformed us from that pale, thin Pommie look to the glowing image of the well-fed Kiwi. It was really grouse!

The medical centre was not far from James' marble yard. One lunchtime I paid James an unexpected visit. Tony came scuttling out of his office to say hello. He wore a smart black suit with a white shirt and a tie. They were the sort of clothes I would normally find attractive, like fine wrapping paper around a present. But I now knew intimately what was underneath – that grotesque hairy body. 'How about lunch?' he asked with a knowing wink.

'No thanks,' I answered. 'I've made meself some sandwiches.'

James came over covered in white marble dust. He wiped his face on a cloth and gave me a quick kiss.

'Yer forgot yer sandwiches this mornin,' I said, giving him the plastic bread-bag. James wiped himself down and we took off to share our sandwiches together in a park across the road.

'Don't be too long, remember he only gets half an hour for lunch!' Tony called.

He thought he was being witty, but it saddened me how he could treat James so shabbily. I thought of telling Sylvia about the motel. But they were probably one of those couples who enoyed an open marriage, and I'd only be adding a bit more amusement to their boring lives.

Pam, one of the younger women I worked with, was a Maori. Almost every weekend she would go up north to be with her extended family. I really envied her close family ties, her sense of belonging. I thought about my own future children. They would have no relatives in the whole Southern Hemisphere: no grandparents, no uncles or aunts, and no cousins. Sometimes the homesickness would return for a short time, then I'd bake an extra-rich chocolate fudge cake or fill a Tupperware container full of rum truffles to distract the sadness. And as long as I didn't look at any photographs from home, I could cope.

Soon we had enough money saved for a deposit on a house. But James desperately wanted what all fishermen eventually want: a boat. We made a deal. James could buy a boat and sail it as long as I wasn't pregnant. As soon as a baby was on the way, he agreed to sell the boat and use the money as a deposit on a house. Naturally, it was in my interest to make sure James' regular activity continued regarding his marital duty. But each month it was the same scarlet discovery, followed by tears of frustration. The time had come to visit a doctor.

The doctor asked lots of questions, writing everything I answered into a file. As his hairy hands scribbled away I tried to read the upside-down words, but they were indecipherable. From working at a medical centre, I'd discovered that doctors tend only to write in Sanskrit anyway. At last he put his pen down, looked up at me, and declared his diagnosis. Psychological disturbance. 'Just relax and forget about babies for a while,' he advised. It was easier to say than to put into practice, but I decided to give it a go.

James bought an eight-metre yacht and we became good Kiwi yachties. I threw myself into baking and boating. While James attended nightschool for a boatmasters course, I learned how to touch-type.

Our weekends were now spent sailing up and down the Hauraki Gulf. Although I still felt seasick much of the time, I enjoyed the sensation of salt spray in my face and the feeling of space and freedom only the sea can provide. James took his new role very seriously, even wearing a navy blue cap saying

CAPTAIN. When he instructed me to point the boat to starboard, I'd feign ignorance out of sheer mischief. 'Right or left?' I'd ask. Or if he used the nautical terms of aft or forward, I'd inquire if he meant the front or the back of the boat. His long-suffering sighs were usually followed by laughter as we played the game of Patient Captain and Useless Crew.

James tried to organise a weekend's sailing with Tony and Sylvia, our boats meeting up at Rakino Island, but I objected. I didn't like the idea of Tony's huge yacht anchored next to our little one. Nor did I relish his winking and innuendo about lunches. James really admired Tony, thinking him a good boss and a good friend. He couldn't understand why I didn't like him. And I couldn't possibly tell him the truth. Or maybe I could.

17

Kawau

The day was unusually still. The sky and sea merged together as one, as though collaborating in some sinister plan. On the boat my every movement seemed to be in slow motion. It was so quiet in all this encompassing blue: no sun, no sparkle on the water, just blue all around us, as though we'd been painted into a picture, and our boat was now an object set against an azure background for all eternity.

Suddenly the water came to life. Something in the distance was moving at a terrific speed, straight at us. Why I'd not noticed before, I don't know, but James was in the water and I was alone on the boat. I tried to call out to James, but I'd become mute.

Then I saw it. A huge killer whale. James was still in the water, and I watched in terror as the great black-and-white orca forged ahead, straight for him. I heard the cracking of human bones first, then James' scream. The creature leaped into the air with James in its mouth. Blood spurted from my husband's eyes and poured from his mouth. The screaming turned to a gurgling sound, and the blueness of the water became red.

I woke up rigid with fright, thankful to find myself in our familiar double bed. The fear I'd experienced in the dream stayed with me, and it took a while for my heart to stop pounding and my body to stop trembling. James continued to sleep peacefully. He was warm and soft to cuddle up to, and his gentle rhythmical snoring was a reassuring sound. Gradually I fell back to sleep.

All the following day the vividness of the dream haunted me. It was the Friday before a long weekend (Monday being a statutory holiday) and we had plans to sail to Kawau, an island about 40 kilometres north of Auckland. At the entrance to Kawau's Bon Accord harbour, killer whales had recently been sighted. It had been on the news.

The terrrifying images of the dream played over and over in my mind as I typed out medical reports on adenocarcinomas, dermatofibromas and epithelial cells. The horrible sound of James' high-pitched scream as the orca's teeth crushed his bones continued to distract me. My typing was full of errors. Hoping the weather would deteriorate, I repeatedly asked my colleagues about the latest forecast for the weekend. But they all made the same prediction. Warm and sunny.

The dream had such an emotional impact on me I decided it could only be a premonition. A terrible warning that must be heeded. Somehow, I had to persuade James that we must not go sailing this weekend, especially not to Kawau.

On the bus journey home I thought of plans and contingency plans. There would be no point in telling James about the dream. He would only scoff and ridicule my female intuition, calling it superstitious hysteria. There was only one course of action to take, I would have to become ill. Very ill.

I was surprised to find James was home before me, and there was no van in the driveway. 'Why are yer home this early?' I asked, patting Lucy who was always pleased to see me. But something was wrong. James was slumped in an armchair, one side of his head held against his hand. He didn't acknowledge me. 'What is it?' I demanded, kneeling down before him. He slowly sat upright and told me he'd been sacked from his job. There had been a disagreement between him and Tony, and Tony had fired him. 'What was it about?' I asked, hoping it wasn't over anything too personal.

'Marble,' he answered. 'He suddenly decided he didn't like my work. My rosework.'

'What a bastard!' I said, my initial shock turning to anger. But then something registered in my mind. Within the flash of a second, something clicked. 'What was he wearin'?' I asked. 'When he sacked yer, was he wearin' his black suit and a white shirt?'

'Don't ask stupid questions!' snapped James, resuming his slumped position.

'But tell me,' I persisted. 'Just say yes or no.' He finally answered. And the answer was yes.

We had a good sail up to Kawau that weekend – me, James and Lucy. It was warm and sunny and we enjoyed a nice little south-westerly all the way up the coast. And after three days away on the boat, James felt a bit happier. He started the new week looking for a new job.

James took a job as a petrol-pump attendant while he waited for something more in line with his trade. Marble masons were not in high demand. People in New Zealand weren't dying off as quickly as the British, and cremation was becoming more popular than burials.

James took his dismissal very hard. It was only our weekends away sailing that brought some joy to his world. But I was still desperate to become pregnant, knowing it would result in James having to sell his beloved boat. It was a dilemma all right.

I decided to go back to the doctor. For months I'd been making a conscious effort to relax and enjoy myself, and forget about babies. I'd done more sailing than Francis Chichester and enough baking to open a cake shop, but there had been no pay off. I was still not pregnant. James refused to accompany me to discuss our infertility problem, insisting there was nothing wrong with his virility.

This time the doctor examined me. I'd never had an internal examination before and I found it embarrassing. I wondered what he could see up there, his gloved fingers prodding about inside me, while I, the real me, lay somewhere further up the couch, not really part of it all. A great spotlight was moved in place. I wondered if a flashlight on a helmet would be more practical, but probably not. It was humiliating enough without feeling like a coalmine. I watched the second hand of the clock going round and round. What was it he could see in that dark and mysterious place? A magic place where all of humanity originated.

At last he turned the light off, removed his gloves and lightly slapped my leg, indicating the examination was over. 'Was everything normal?' I asked, not liking the expression on his face. He said he wasn't sure and would like to send me to a specialist. I felt a combination of relief and fear. At least a specialist could tell us what the problem was.

At work, Pam informed us she had become pregnant. We helped her celebrate by all bringing in a Friday Treat on the same Friday, pigging out on Pavlova, brandy snaps, cheesecake and glasses of Chardon. I never mentioned the frustrated months and years I had spent trying to conceive.

Barbara, an older woman, began to read our palms. She had taught herself the art of palmistry by reading step-by-step instructions in the *New Zealand Woman's Weekly*. She knew all about lifelines and heartlines, saying Pam would move away from Auckland soon, and her child would be a boy, the first of three. 'And what about me?' I asked, holding out an upturned hand. She could see some travel, maybe to America. And an unexpected inheritance of some sort. But I wasn't interested in travelling or money. 'What about kids?' She said she could see two children, a boy and a girl. 'When?' It wasn't to be too far off. Maybe in two years. I was pleased to hear it, but two years! That was a long time to wait. We all knew Barbara's predictions were only a bit of fun, but I certainly didn't want to wait a couple of years for a baby.

I volunteered to eat the last piece of Pavlova, and focused my attention on Pam's body. I too would soon be in that condition. And for my celebration I decided on chocolate truffles, fudge cake, strawberry meringues and glasses of Cold Duck. Yes, it was just a matter of time now.

Nothing prepared me for the shocking news I received after my second visit to the specialist. I could never have children. Pelvic inflammatory disease had left my fallopian tubes damaged beyond repair. How this silent damage occurred was a mystery. The specialist put it down to a viral infection in childhood. She had wanted James to be there when she told me, but he wouldn't come. Women's gynaecological problems were for women. I was offered counselling, but I refused.

In a daze, I wandered towards the bus stop, hoping I would soon wake up to find it was only a dream. Instead of going home I found myself in a pet-shop, buying a kitten. It was a black-and-white male with white whiskers and paws, and a dear little face. I put him inside my jacket and ordered a taxi home.

I didn't tell James. How do you tell a man he's bought damaged goods? Especially when he had been pressured into the purchase.

I called the kitten Mitty. James had gone away sailing for the weekend while I settled Mitty into his new home. Lucy was very inquisitive. Her huge nose sniffed and studied the new resident, and the tiny cat hissed back. Soon they became acquainted, and the sniffing and hissing subsided.

The yellow bootees I'd bought years ago lay unwrapped on the bed. No baby's feet of mine would ever wear them. I felt so numb, I couldn't even cry. As a ceremonial gesture I dug a hole in the back garden and buried the bootees. All the other baby things I'd collected over the years – the lace bib, the matinee jackets, the little blue hairbrush – I decided to give to Pam at work.

Later that day, the bootees, torn and muddy, were given back to me by Lucy. She'd dug them up and carried them into the house, dropping them onto my lap as I sat staring at the unplugged TV. The tears came in a flood. Lucy whined along with me, nuzzling my face for comfort. And she did give comfort. It's hard to continue crying with a dog's high-pitched whine drowning out your own sobs. The kitten nestled into my lap and purred while Lucy badgered at my hand for strokes. Lucy was a love junkie now.

Feeling better, I decided to burn the bootees and try to begin yet another new life. But I had to tell James. It was hard to predict how he'd react on hearing that his wife was now officially barren. Barren. I was now a barren woman. It conjured up images of a dry, infertile desert. A useless womb. Nature's basic intention is for all living things to reproduce, and I couldn't even do that.

The sky was growing dark. It was almost six o'clock and James would soon be home. I made a meal of spaghetti Bolognese and prepared myself to reveal the shattering news. At least he could keep his boat.

18

The Pack

Molly was a droopy-eared shaggy little mongrel. Unlike Lucy, her cheeky personality still sparkled, even in the dim squalor of the Auckland Dog Pound. When I first saw her she reminded me of Moll Flanders in Newgate Prison, the type of inmate who was destined to eventually find a good home, in Torbay if not Virginia. When the vet examined Molly he told me she was much more than meets the eye. Without knowing it I'd taken home nine dogs – Molly and an unborn litter of eight pups. For practical reasons the pups were aborted and the wayward Molly was speyed.

At home a new hierarchy struggled into existence. Poor Lucy remained at the bottom of the pecking order. She was a gentle giant, bossed about by Mitt the moggy, and now by Molly the mongrel. On discovering we owned two dogs, the landlord ordered us to leave. It was a time of upheaval anyway. James was becoming disillusioned with New Zealand. He wasn't able to find a job as a marble mason anywhere in Auckland and suspected Tony of malicious slander. He accepted my infertility far better than I'd anticipated, although I think his view of the situation didn't extend beyond short term.

There were changes in our marriage too. Because there was no chance of becoming pregnant, my interest in sexual activity gradually diminished. There was no point to it. Our relationship became platonic, and James spent most weekends on his boat, while I enjoyed the company of my animals.

Our next house was in Browns Bay. The previous residents had left us a surprise gift, their fluffy ginger tom cat. Edgar became pet number four. He was a very relaxed cat, a complete gentleman who didn't mind the strange people and animals moving into his territory. As long as his foodbowl was filled twice a day and there was an empty space by the fire, he was happy enough. At last Lucy moved up a notch in the hierarchy, and the humble Edgar settled into his place at the bottom.

But James couldn't settle. His restless spirit was now wanting to emigrate to Canada, saying Vancouver was the most beautiful city in the world. It had a harbour and it snowed at Christmas, so what were we waiting for? But emigrating to Canada had no appeal for me. Besides, how could I leave my beloved pets? Did he really think we could put Lucy and Molly back on Death Row, and throw the cats out onto the street?

The following September, James left for Vancouver and I stayed with my family of cats and dogs. It was strange at first, not having James around. He rang a few times, begging me to join him in the 'marvellous new place' and I almost did. Almost. But I decided it wasn't fair on James. Why should he be denied the pleasures of fatherhood because of some lousy viral infection in my childhood? Gradually the calls tapered off and one morning the inevitable divorce papers arrived in the post. I heard later that he remarried and had two children. And another boat.

Remaining alone in the Southern Hemisphere, I made my

world among the canine and feline species. I was an important and popular member of The Pack. Each evening when I returned home from work, I received the best greeting anybody could ever wish for. I cuddled them, talked to them in a high-pitched voice, scolded them and sang to them. And they returned an emotional dividend tenfold. After tea we'd all make ourselves cosy on a large settee: me, two dogs and two cats. There was always the inital competition, when four personalities vied for best position, but it was always Molly who managed to push her head into my lap. After the growling and hissing ceased, and each animal settled into a position appropriate to its status, the harmonious sound of purring and contented dog-mutterings could be heard between the tracks of music. We enjoyed listening to Bach's fugues (the organ music that had frightened me so long ago at church), while I sipped a couple of glasses of Australian dry red.

I was never lonely, except when I thought of my family in Liverpool, and I never felt the need for a man. I found company enough in my animals, and through colleagues at work and my women friends. At work, the women seemed to believe me when I said I'd chosen not to have children, that there were enough human beings on earth without me adding more. Repeating this statement so often to others I came to believe it myself.

As my genes wouldn't be making it into the future, I gradually began to look back to the past. Early New Zealand Maori wore their family history on their face and body in the form of the *moko*. My history was only linked to a name I'd discarded so passionately long ago. For a moment, I even considered taking it back. After experiencing years of ridicule in my most sensitive years, surely a more mature me could now handle the remarks. Instead of feeling ashamed, I could say 'Yes, it is an amusing name, an old English name, but d'you know what, it's absolutely unique!' I toyed with this idea for a while, but decided to stay with the meaningless sound of Mortimer.

> She lived unknown, and few could know
> When Lucy ceased to be;
> But she is in her grave, and, oh,
> The difference to me!
> William Wordsworth

When Lucy died I was heartbroken for weeks. She was replaced by Lucy Two, another Alsatian bitch who quickly became Lutu. Old Mitt was replaced by Willow. The living room wall became a gallery of portraits, my family of dogs and cats. At each death, the terrible sorrow would be followed by the renewed joy of settling in another pet.

It was a strange and perhaps pathetic way to live, but it suited me. I never stopped missing my mum and sisters back home, though. The young girl who emigrated had left her severed roots in the old country; roots that still lingered beneath the soil, continually flowering in a cycle of sorrow and happiness.

19

Digestive Tubes

There are three powerfully evocative smells in this world – the fragrance of wild jasmine wafting on a September breeze in Auckland, the salty maritime smell of the River Mersey at the Pier Head in Liverpool, and the sharp exciting smell of straight gin, anytime, anywhere. But this morning, outside Mangere Airport, there was nothing powerful nor evocative to be smelt on the breeze, even though it is September, and the beginning of spring. The large Samoan taxi driver in dark glasses had stood waiting, tapping his fat impatient fingers on the car roof. I'd arrived at the airport in a bit of a fluster. The taxi was held up by roadworks in Onehunga and my purse had somehow been packed away in the suitcase instead of in my shoulder bag. I finally came across the small black purse, its bundle of New Zealand dollars, British pounds and Hong Kong dollars, placed in different compartments. I gave the driver an extra two dollars for making him wait. Then, with a sense of rising panic, I lugged my suitcases over to join one of the check-in queues for my flight to Hong Kong.

Airports are strange places. Falsely cool, echoing with human noise and intimidating, where the clock and the official stamp are gods. Everybody waiting to be somewhere else. Nobody being here now. That's one of those comforting sayings from the sensible seventies – be here now. So standing in the queue for the ticket counter, I try to be here now as this too will soon pass, but it's not easy.

I recall leaving Liverpool many years ago, and arriving as an immigrant in Auckland. It was a cold Wednesday morning in August, and a strong southerly was blowing up from the Antarctic with driving rain. We were expecting sub-tropical weather and lots of sheep. The song 'Barbados' was in the charts, and the song had beat its special rhythm inside my head during the long journey. The three syllables of Bar-bad-os were replaced by New-Zea-land and sung with the same sunny Caribbean accent: 'Oh! I'm going to New Zealand'. James wore a white suit and I wore a sleeveless yellow dress. We were very naive, and slightly disappointed when we saw our new city, Auckland – the city of sails. The cosmopolitan metropolis of New Zealand which was to be our new home in the Southern Hemisphere, 'far away from Liv-er-pool, and de rain'.

So here I am once more at Auckland International airport, in suspended animation waiting to be checked in, approved and stamped. I'm about to undergo a long flight back to England to see my family, and I have to be strong, or at least appear to be. My mum and sisters still won't be into showing emotion or affection like most women. Hello, goodbye, smiling, full of light banter, but no touching and no tears. I wonder again if they're really like me, hiding their aching hearts behind a grinning mask, but I can't be sure. It's always been safer to go along with the comedy than be revealed as weak. Although a family of females, we behave like a gathering of staunch men.

A Dandelion By Any Other Name

Eventually I find myself inside a DC10, destination Hong Kong. I'm booked to stop over for two nights before flying on to Manchester. The plane moves smoothly down the runway and then the whole 250 tonnes of aeroplane lifts heavily and jerkily into the air. From the window, the city below is transformed into small fragmented shapes. I say a silent farewell to Auckland, my new home, with its magnificent west coast beaches of black glittering sand and white exploding surf. Goodbye beautiful Aotearoa, land of the long white cloud. I will return.

The 'fasten seatbelts' light goes out and people start to relax. Already the trolley of drinks is rattling down the aisle. The task of feeding and watering the passengers begins. Pour it in one end and squeeze it out the other. Like worms, we will wriggle about in between feeds, wondering what the next trolley will bring. Was Cabanis right in saying man is but a digestive tube? I bet Beethoven often forgot to eat during the creation of a symphony, and I can't imagine Coleridge putting down the first few lines of Kubla Khan for a cup of tea and a sandwich. But he might have.

Is it any wonder I'm partial to a spot of gin? This is the question on my mind as I nibble my peanuts and sip a gin and tonic. The smell of gin always reminds me of my mum. Not because it's called Mother's Ruin, nor that she is or ever was an alcoholic. You see, before I was born, my poor mum tried to exterminate me. She drank half a bottle of the stuff while sitting in a hot mustard bath. That's the sort of thing they did in those days. Needless to say, it didn't work. 'Yer were determined to be born,' she told me. 'The gin nor the mustard couldn't shift yer.'

She never made a secret of this fact, even when I was a young child. It was something we all laughed at – Deirdre, the stubborn baby. And I laughed too. I was even born a Taurean, renowned for being stubborn, but sometimes under the blankets at night, things didn't seem that funny. But I was little then and didn't understand properly. My mother had been young, pregnant and unmarried. She'd tried to escape her socially unacceptable condition by attempting to rid herself of the problem and it didn't work. It was as simple as that.

I finish off my drink and gently rattle the ice cubes around the empty glass. Oh yes, I've always been very fond of gin.

'...the temperature in Hong Kong is currently thirty-one degrees with around ninety percent humidity. Local time is four-thirty in the afternoon.' I am about to land in the Far East. Outside only grey cloud is visible as the plane is buffeted from side to side by a tropical storm. Passengers observe each other to check impressions and expressions. Their fear only shows in widened eyes, and mouths forming an oooh shape before changing into a shrugging smile. Social norms allow us this. Hysteria is fastened down along with our seatbelts. The trays have been put neatly away, our seats are in the upright position and we wait. Heads with frightened simpering faces turn from window across to window as we sit and wait to be safe.

It's now thundering loudly as the plane lowers its enormous body in search of a runway. Through the window there are violent flashes of lightning. Straining my neck to look down, I catch a glimpse of the city, a miniature New York, set against a dingy yellow sky. The lights go out and we are quiet. It's the uncomfortable human quiet experienced just prior to landing. The fury of the storm accentuates it even more. We wait and listen for the anticipated smooth bump of the wheels on the runway. In Hong Kong the airport is next to the sea. The landing is slightly bumpy, but I feel grateful to the pilot. It's the same gratitude we reserve for surgeons. Our life has been in their hands

A Dandelion By Any Other Name

and they haven't bungled.

At 1am Hong Kong time I'm tucked up alone in a strange bed. It's kingsize, but I still keep to my side, the left side. Although tired, sleep will not come. The air conditioning is noisy and chills the room. People say you can sleep better when it's cool. Maybe that's true, but it's something to do with loneliness that's keeping me awake. When I spread my arm out over the great expanse of the bed, nobody's there. Saying a mantra doesn't help – my mind's like a wild animal that can't be tamed. I turn the light on and read, but my eyes are smarting, still feeling dried out from the flight.

I can only read a couple of pages, something about the Greek philosopher Socrates. He reckoned that the unexamined life is not worth living. I quickly put the book away and turn the light off again. Yes, I think old Socrates is probably right.

Even at 8am the harbour is full of movement. Ferry boats and sampans sail up and down the murky water. Already my body's sweating with the hot, damp air as we cruise past the docks. I imagine what Hong Kong must have looked like in the 1930s, when my dad lived here for three years. He must have sailed into this harbour when he was a young man, looked up and observed the city surrounded by the same misty hills. My eyes start to well with tears. It's hard to imagine him being a young man; he was only ever my old whiskery, grumpy dad. I wish now I could have shown him some affection while he was alive. He didn't get much.

After the cruise, walking along the pier, I watch a small elderly woman. Her right hand pulls a trolley full of domestic bundles. Her other hand is held out in a begging gesture. She only seems to approach men, her eyes staring ahead without the act of looking. She walks up to one white male tourist and then another. I wonder why she seems to avoid asking anything of women.

Perhaps she is an ageing prostitute and is only used to taking money from men. Or maybe experience has told her that men tend to be more charitable, more willing to give. I ferret about in my purse for something to give her but when I look up she has crossed the road. A couple of policemen walk past. Maybe begging is against the law here.

In the early afternoon it's very hot. I ride on a little wooden train to the summit of Mount Victoria. The view of the city is fascinating. It really is like a smaller, more exotic version of New York. The steaming green hills all around enclose it like a shrine to the Far East. Where my dad, Mr Harold William Rammsbottom, once lived. The South China Sea, The Orient, Typhoons, Chicken Chow Mein and Tiger Balm. Such exotic sounds!

Shopping is not as exciting as I'd anticipated. Streets are crowded and shopkeepers stand menacingly outside their shops. It feels intimidating. To look in a shop window is to be harassed. There are hardly any prices on anything. To buy even an apple, requires haggling over a price and I don't like haggling, so I go without.

After a full day in Hong Kong I start to feel weary of being a tourist. The evening air is now so humid it feels as though you're breathing in steam. I eat a quick meal then take a taxi back to my hotel. After a leisurely bath, I climb into the huge bed and fall asleep right away. In a dream, my mum is visiting me in New Zealand. She's slumped in an armchair feeling sick. Her cheeks are flushed and her eyes half closed. I feel very maternal towards her. I want to comfort and support her, but she waves me away with her hand.

I wake up still feeling the emotion from the dream. After a little weep, I make a resolution: this time, when I arrive in England, I'm going to hug and kiss my mother. Even if she reels in horror, I'm going to do it, for me. I might even try it on my sisters too. I get up out of bed and write the resolution in my little notebook. Once something is written, it becomes a law. And I am the law keeper.

20

Arriving

Seatbelts are fastened and headrests are being adjusted to the upright position. The original homeland now lies below. England – the land of my birth. Soon I'll be landing at Manchester airport and meeting my family again. The thought of hugging and kissing them makes me feel nervous. They'll wonder what's wrong with me and feel embarrassed. But I've made a promise to myself, and I must carry it out, even though it won't be appreciated or reciprocated.

But she might not turn up. My mum's routine is very important to her. If *Coronation Street* or *Eastenders* is on TV, or there are 'good prizes' at the local bingo hall that day, the interruption caused by my arrival will be annoying. Very annoying.

Although there's a certain comfort in knowing where you stand in the scheme of things. Obviously for me it's after *Coronation Street*, *Eastenders* and the bingo. Oh yes, I know my place.

They'll already be there, waiting for me in the arrival area. I imagine how they might look: Janet, with her familiar frown reading the flight information; Cushla, dressed in some fashionable outfit (anticipating the envious remark, which will of course be obliged), and my mum (if she turns up), slouching on a seat, her grey head hidden between the pages of a daily newspaper, the sort with sleazy headlines such as 'VICAR CAUGHT IN KINKY SEX ROMP!'

This time will be different. This time there is a mission to be accomplished. The mission may seem a simple natural act, but it isn't. I'm going to hug and kiss my mother and sisters. No doubt their first reaction will be as passive receivers of this shock treatment, this unnatural act which will prove disturbing and embarrassing, but which must be done.

They'll try to fend me off with the old currency – chocolate. Packets of new confectionery products will be put in my arms, and little chocolate squares with interesting flavours will be placed in my mouth. Our expressions of family love – or if not love, then certainly affection – must now change and be acknowledged in a new form, that of the embrace. The old value system has long gone stale and must be thrown out. A time for renewal and reconstruction has come.

There is a special technique I've evolved for performing tasks that would be easier avoided. There's an old woman sitting in an old folks' home. Her head has fallen to one side, leaning awkwardly on her shoulder while saliva continually trickles down the side of her chin and onto her clothes. She counts the minutes and hours, drop by drop. It has become her new timekeeper. The only thing in life she now has to look forward to is *Coronation Street* on TV. That old woman is me projected into the future. And she's content to be in that state as long as she hasn't lived a lifetime of avoidance, finding her soul immobilised at the end of a long journey, and a heart full of regrets. She wants good memories to fall back on for those days – memories of courageous action and the taste of experience, not a bag of 'if onlys' and putting off.

A few months ago, I was teetering on the top diving board at a local swimming centre. I wanted to jump, to feel the experience, but it seemed so high. I was afraid and my body became paralysed. And guess who came to my aid that day? It was that old dribbling woman. She pushed me off the board, gathered up the feeling of rushing adrenalin as I fell through the air, and invested it in her memory bank for the years ahead. And she'll feed upon that experience in the old folks' home, while the dribble slowly drops.

Very soon that same old woman (she has been invited) will be with me at the Manchester arrival area, when I embrace three very important people. She'll be there to supervise and make sure I accomplish the difficult task that's been set.

We land. The 'fasten seatbelt' lights go out and the plane suddenly becomes animated with people putting on jackets, opening lockers, pulling down bundles and lifting up bags. The movement has a unique sound: humanity raring to go, the bustle of people wanting to get on with their lives, as though we had been on hold for a few days.

Being in a window seat, there's not much point in standing up yet, especially as my blond neighbour is still struggling with her shoes and swollen feet.

'Can I pass you ladies anything?' The voice belongs to an Irishman from the seat in front. He's standing up, one hand in our overhead locker as he looks at us for acknowledgement. A yellow-and-green sleeve dangles down like a woollen snake. The blond woman asks for her bag of duty-free and jacket. I ask him if he could pass me my black travel bag.

'There's two black bags here,' he says, showing me one of them.

'Is this one yours?'

'No,' I tell him, 'it must be the other. It should have the name Rammsbottom on it. Deirdre Rammsbottom. With three M's.'

The Irishman's expression doesn't change as he lifts down my bag, nor does the woman's next to me. After experiencing a 'normal' surname, I have now changed back to my original. Janet and Cushla think I'm crazy to resume the burden I so vigorously tried to cast off. Perhaps they're right.

You see, there are now only two people left in the world with that particular name. My mum and me. Two women on the verge of extinction. We are outside the comforts of the fold, and it's taken over forty years for me to realise that the fold is not as comfortable as it appears. My mum and I are now joined together by name, a relationship no man will ever put asunder.

Yes, I finally decided to take the old name back after all, and yes, it is amusing, it's an old English name, and d'you know what, it's absolutely unique! And what is in a name? Clanship perhaps, a sense of belonging? Cushla married but chose not to have children. Janet never married but spent her life devoted to her son. And my mum, well she still watches *Coronation Street*.

Socrates once said that the unexamined life is not worth living. Maybe he was right. But I've discovered an opposing philosophical view: Digestive Tubes have more fun! A new saying for the nineties?

'Thank you very much,' I say to the Irishman as I take my bag.

'You're most welcome,' he answers in a pleasant lilting brogue, pleased to be helpful. 'You ladies have a nice trip,' he calls as he navigates his way amongst the confusion of passengers down the aisle.

Yes, I will have a nice trip. The best yet.